BUNNICULA
Fun Book

BUNNICULA
Fun Book

JAMES HOWE
Illustrated by Alan Daniel

Morrow Junior Books/New York

Text excerpts on pages 2, 6, and 104 from *Bunnicula: A Rabbit-Tale of Mystery* by Deborah and James Howe, copyright © 1979 by James Howe; pages 26 and 104 from *The Celery Stalks at Midnight* by James Howe, copyright © 1983 by James Howe; pages 92 and 104 from *Howliday Inn* by James Howe, copyright © 1982 by James Howe; pages 76, 105, and 150 from *Nighty-Nightmare* by James Howe, text copyright © 1987 by James Howe; pages 98 and 105 from *Return to Howliday Inn* by James Howe, text copyright © 1992 by James Howe. All of the above books were published by Atheneum, New York.

Text excerpts on pages 18 and 105 from *Creepy-Crawly Birthday* by James Howe, text copyright © 1991 by James Howe; pages 104 and 120 from *The Fright Before Christmas* by James Howe, text copyright © 1988 by James Howe; page 105 and Mr. Monroe's Famous Fudge recipe on pages 54-55 from *Hot Fudge* by James Howe, text copyright © 1990 by James Howe; page 105 and the "Rabbit-Cadabra!" Magic Trick on pages 32-40 from *Rabbit-Cadabra!* by James Howe, text copyright © 1993 by James Howe (The "Rabbit-Cadabra!" Magic Trick was created by Martin J. Schwartz D.D.S. In addition to practicing general dentistry in New York City, Dr. Schwartz is an inventor and manufacturer of magic tricks.); pages 104 and 120 from *Scared Silly: A Halloween Treat* by James Howe, text copyright © 1989 by James Howe. All of the above books were published by Morrow Junior Books, New York.

Permission to use the following photographs and illustrations is gratefully acknowledged: page 47, courtesy of Dan Curtis Productions; page 100, from page 19 of *Peter Rabbit* by Beatrix Potter (London, 1902), courtesy of Frederick Warne, Inc., copyright © 1902, 1987; page 131, copyright © Touchstone Pictures/Amblin Entertainment. The illustration on page 91 originally appeared in *Uncle Remus* by Joel Chandler Harris, illustrated by A.B. Frost.

Text copyright © 1993 by James Howe
Illustrations copyright © 1993 by Alan Daniel

Printed in the United States of America.

1 2 3 4 5 6 7 8 9 10

ISBN 0-688-11952-2 (pbk.)
LC 92-34561

Acknowledgments

The *Bunnicula Fun Book* represents the efforts of a number of people besides myself. I would like to thank my editors at Morrow Junior Books, Andrea Curley and David Reuther, as well as editorial assistant Michael Street and art director Barbara Fitzsimmons, for all their hard work and creativity. I also wish to thank Ann Naughton's fifth-grade class, 1991–92, at Hillside Elementary School, Hastings-on-Hudson, New York, for their good ideas and valuable feedback. The staff of Good Yarns Bookstore in Hastings as well as the librarians at the Hastings Public Library were always ready with suggestions and help, for which I am grateful. Thanks, too, to Nancy Carver and, as always, to my wife, Betsy Imershein, and my daughter, Zoe.

—JAMES HOWE

Contents

WORD GAMES

SCRAMBLED SQUARES

WORD FINDS

WRITE ON!

EDITOR'S NOTE

If you've read any of the Bunnicula books, you know that Harold, a dog, writes them. This book is different. As Harold put it to me over lunch at his favorite restaurant, Le Plat de Chien, "Why should I have all the fun? I know my readers enjoy my adventures with Chester and Howie and Bunnicula, but why shouldn't they get in on the action? Wouldn't it be great if there were a book in which they could do some of the writing?

"Maybe there could be fun things in it like some puzzles and trivia quizzes, a few jokes (Howie could come up with those), a yummy recipe (Mr. Monroe's fudge, mmmm!), a magic trick, pages for drawing . . ." Harold would have gone on, but he was distracted by the sight of an approaching dessert cart.

I thought Harold's idea was terrific, so after lunch I called up his friend and collaborator, James Howe, to see if he agreed. "I love it!" the voice on the other end of the phone exclaimed. "A fun book like this is perfect for rainy days at home, long car trips, vacations, sleepaway camp. It's something to do between books, after homework, instead of TV . . ." His voice trailed off, and I soon heard the sound of computer keys clicking away. He was already at work.

Now his work is done and your fun is about to begin! You'll have a good time with the *Bunnicula Fun Book* anyway you go about it. Start at the beginning or pick a page at random, find something that sounds like fun from the table of contents—just choose the activity you feel like doing when you feel like doing it. You can't go wrong. You don't even need to have read the other Bunnicula books to have a great time with this one. All you need is a pencil, a sense of humor, and a lively imagination.

Have fun!

—THE EDITOR

A-maze-ing!

Help Bunnicula
Get to the Salad Bowl

"I know what you're doing, Chester, and the jig is up. That little bunny never hurt anybody. All he's doing is eating his own way. What do you care if he drains a few vegetables?"

"He's a vampire!" Chester snarled. "Today, vegetables. Tomorrow . . . the world!"

—*from* Bunnicula: A Rabbit-Tale of Mystery

Bunnicula's hungry, and there's nothing to get in the way between him and a big bowl of crispy green vegetables. Nothing, that is, except Chester, who will use any means to rid the world of the vegetarian vampire rabbit. Keep Bunnicula away from Chester's garlic and water traps—both deadly to vampires—and whatever you do, don't let Chester get him.

There's only one safe path to the salad bowl. Can you help Bunnicula find it?

The solution appears on page 155.

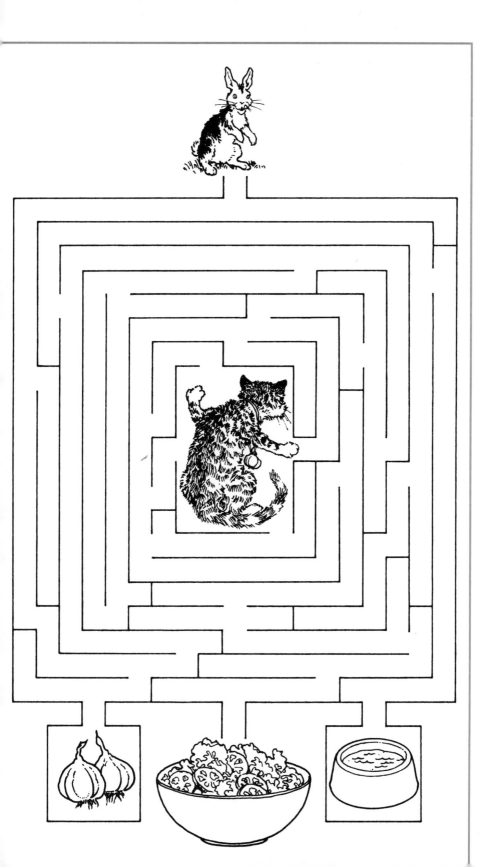

Chester's Magic Hat Puzzle

E ach word on the left holds one letter in a magic hat. The clue on the right will help you to fill in the blanks and find the magic letters. After you've pulled all the letters from the hats, put them in the spaces at the bottom to answer one more puzzle: What is **Chester's battle cry**?

The solutions appear on page 156.

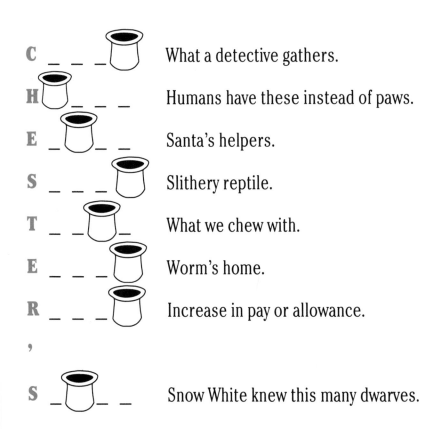

C _ _ _ What a detective gathers.

H _ _ _ Humans have these instead of paws.

E _ _ _ _ Santa's helpers.

S _ _ _ _ Slithery reptile.

T _ _ _ _ What we chew with.

E _ _ _ _ Worm's home.

R _ _ _ _ Increase in pay or allowance.

'

S _ _ _ _ Snow White knew this many dwarves.

4

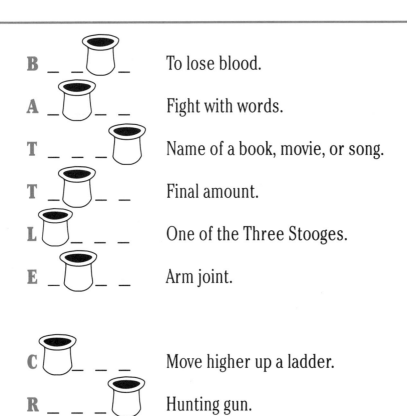

B _ _ _ _   To lose blood.

A _ _ _ _   Fight with words.

T _ _ _ _   Name of a book, movie, or song.

T _ _ _ _   Final amount.

L _ _ _ _   One of the Three Stooges.

E _ _ _ _   Arm joint.

C _ _ _   Move higher up a ladder.

R _ _ _ _   Hunting gun.

Y _ _ _   A decade has ten.

Chester's Battle Cry:

_ _ _ _   _ _ _

_ _ _ _ _ _ _ _ _ _ !!

5

Write On!

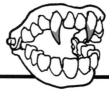

If I Were a Vampire . . .

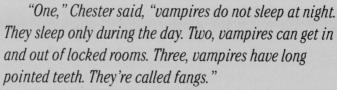

"One," Chester said, "vampires do not sleep at night. They sleep only during the day. Two, vampires can get in and out of locked rooms. Three, vampires have long pointed teeth. They're called fangs."

"Well, don't we have fangs?"

"No, we have canines. Fangs are more pointed, and vampires use fangs to bite people on the neck."

"Yech! Who'd want to do that?"

"Vampires would, that's who."

—*from* Bunnicula: A Rabbit-Tale of Mystery

Answer these questions as if *you* were a vampire.

My vampire name is: _____

What I like best about being a vampire is: _____

_____

Here's the worst part: _____

_____

_____

The funniest thing that ever happened to me was the time:

_____

_____

Here's my favorite way to scare people: _____

_____

_____

But one time I was scared. Here's what happened: _____

_____

_____

If I were running for class president, this would be my

campaign slogan: _____

_____

When I write my autobiography, I think I'll title it: _____

_____

My favorite time of day or night is: _____

My favorite place to be is: _____

My favorite snack is: _____

Scrambled Squares

Bunnicula's Cousin?!

The monster pictured below is all mixed up. To figure out who's hiding in these boxes, copy each drawing into the matching numbered box on the opposite page.

The solution appears on page 156.

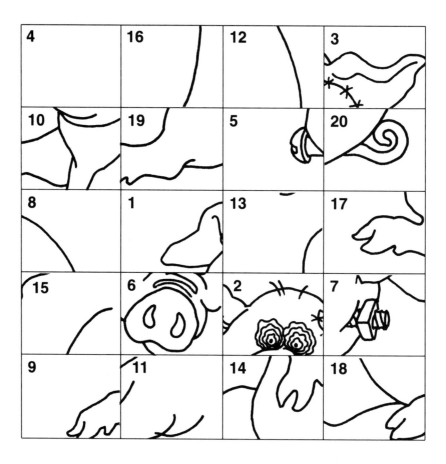

1	2	3	4
5	6	7	8
9	10	11	12
13	14	15	16
17	18	19	20

Count Dracula's Knock-Knock Jokes

These are best when done with a Transylvanian accent!

Knock knock.
> *Who's there?*

Mike.
> *Mike who?*

Mike coffin is filled with dirt!

Knock knock.
> *Who's there?*

Dave.
> *Dave who?*

Dave been trying to destroy Dracula for centuries, but he's still here!

Knock knock.
> *Who's there?*

Ivan.
> *Ivan who?*

Ivan awful craving for your blood!

Knock knock.
Who's there?
Carmen.
Carmen who?
Carmen into my den!

Knock knock.
Who's there?
Jillian.
Jillian who?
Jillian damp in here, isn't it?

Knock knock.
Who's there?
Don.
Don who?
Don take your eyes off me!

Knock knock.
Who's there?
Lucian.
Lucian who?
Lucian your collar so I can
bite your neck!

Knock knock.
   Who's there?
Olive.
   Olive who?
Olive your skin—it's so tender and pale!

Knock knock.
   Who's there?
Justin.
   Justin who?
Justin time for a quick bite!

Knock knock.
   Who's there?
Alex.
   Alex who?
Alex the questions around here!

Knock knock.
Who's there?
Juan.
Juan who?
Juan day you will be mine!

Knock knock.
Who's there?
Diane.
Diane who?
Diane to see me, weren't you?

Knock knock.
Who's there?
Fangs.
Fangs who?
Fangs for dropping by!

Wacky Words!

Wacky Words! is a game that's fun for one person, two people, or the whole gang. If you're playing it alone, fill in the list on the next page with whatever words come to mind. Don't turn the page until you've completed the entire list. *Then* turn the page and fill in the blanks in the story, using the words you've listed here.

If you're playing with others, go directly to page 16. Announce the type of word called for under each blank. Each of the other players takes a turn providing a word that fits. Don't read any of the story aloud until all the blanks are filled in. Then read it from beginning to end—and just try to keep from laughing! The wackiest, funniest, and most descriptive words will give you the wildest, craziest stories!

The Mysterious Note

_____
1. NOUN

_____
2. NOUN

_____
3. PERSON'S NAME

_____
4. BODY PART

_____
5. ANIMAL

_____
6. PERSON'S NAME

_____
7. NOUN

_____
8. PERSON'S NAME

_____
9. NOUN

_____
10. NOUN

_____
11. ANIMAL

_____
12. VERB, PAST TENSE

_____
13. VERB

_____
14. PLURAL NOUN

_____
15. NOUN

_____
16. PLURAL NOUN

_____
17. PLURAL NOUN

_____
18. ANY WORD

_____
19. NOUN

Wacky Words!

The Mysterious Note

One day at school, Toby found a mysterious note taped to

his _____ . It read: "Meet me at the playground
    (1. noun)

after school. Come alone and bring a _____ !" The
                                     (2. noun)

note wasn't signed, but Toby suspected it was the work of

_____ , the class bully. Toby's _____
(3. person's name)   *(4. body part)*

broke into a sweat and he could feel _____
                                         (5. animal)

bumps all over his body. He was scared, but he knew he had

to show up.

All day he thought about the terrible things the bully had

done. He remembered the time _____ 's
                             (6. person's name)

_____ had been put on the school roof and the
    (7. noun)

time _____ 's _____ had been glued to
    (8. person's name)   *(9. noun)*

a _____ . And just last week a live _____
   (10. noun)   *(11. animal)*

had been found in the teacher's desk drawer!

Toby _____ all the way to the playground that
      (12. verb, past tense)

afternoon. He wished he were _____ ing
                                (13. verb)

instead—anything but having to face the bully. But something strange happened. The bully never showed up. "What a relief!" Toby thought. But when he realized how late he was going to get home, he thought, "Oh, no, Mom and Dad will really pop their _____!"

(14. plural noun)

At home, Toby found a second mysterious note. This one read: "We've got you now! Open this door at your own risk!"

Swallowing hard, Toby opened the door—half expecting to find the bully waiting inside with a _____ to

(15. noun)

clobber him.

Instead, he walked into a room full of people. The room was decorated with _____ and _____.

(16. plural noun)   (17. plural noun)

Everyone yelled, " _____ !"

(18. any word)

"A birthday party!" Toby cried. "What a neat surprise!"

But the biggest surprise of all was to see the class bully, who'd even brought a present. "Gee," Toby said when he opened it. "Just what I always wanted: a _____ !"

(19. noun)

Write On!

Birthday Cake and Ice Cream, Too!

> Toby's birthday was here at last. I had been waiting for weeks.
>
> "Toby has the best birthday parties," I said to Chester. "Remember last year?"
>
> Chester licked his whiskers. "Mrs. Monroe left a gallon of ice cream out on the kitchen table," he said dreamily.
>
> —from Creepy-Crawly Birthday

My birthday is: _____

My best birthday ever was: _____

_____

My worst birthday ever was: _____

_____

To me, the perfect birthday party would be: _____

_____

_____

I'm looking forward to my next birthday because:_____

_____

I think the perfect age to be is: _____

**I'm like Harold and Chester and Howie. I
love ice cream.**

My three favorite flavors are: _____

_____   _____

Made-up Flavors

Flavors I wish were real: Silly flavors:

_____   _____

_____   _____

_____   _____

_____   _____

Truly gross flavors:

_____

_____

_____

_____

Pencil Pause

How to Draw Chester

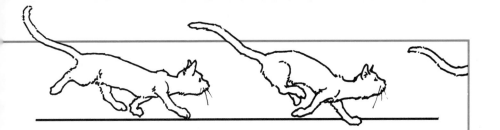

Howie's Howlers

Why can't a rabbit move more than four feet?
> Because it only has four feet.

On which side does a rabbit have more fur?
> The outside.

What wakes bunnies up in the morning?
> Rabbit rousers.

Where do you find rabbits in Paris, France?
> The hutch back of Notre Dame.

What do you call a line of bunnies walking backward?
> A receding hare line.

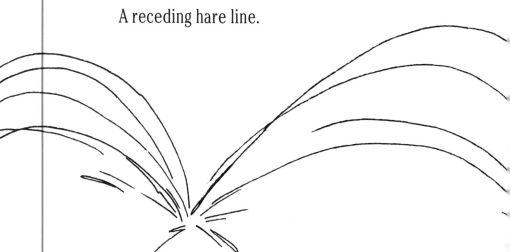

What did the tortoise say after he ran against the rabbit?

"My, that was a hare racing experience!"

What did the rabbit's neighbors say after he was arrested?

"Hare today, con tomorrow."

What do you call a fancy dance for rabbits?

A hare ball.

Why did the rabbit turn down the job at the supermarket?

The celery was too low.

How do bunnies travel?

Rabbit transit.

Funny Bunny

Superstitions About Rabbits

American children may grow up looking for a *man* in the moon, but Japanese children look for a *rabbit*.

In Ancient Egypt, the hare was thought to be a spirit of the dawn and enlightenment. The written symbol, or hieroglyph, for the verb "to exist" was a hare with a ripple of water beneath.

Superstitions connecting rabbits or hares with witches can be found in myths and folklore the world over. The oldest and most widely held belief was that witches transformed themselves into hares. In West Africa, if hare tracks were found, they were dug up, turned over, and buried, in the hope that the witch who inhabited the hare's body would be suffocated.

The luck of the rabbit's foot is the strongest rabbit-related superstition that exists to this day. No one knows exactly how this superstition began, although it is certain that it goes a long way back in time. Something else is certain about this superstition: What's lucky for you and me is unlucky for the rabbit!

According to an Algonquin Indian myth, the Great Hare or "Michabo" is the ruler of the winds and guardian of the people.

PORTUGUESE
CRUISE LINES
COOK ISLANDS ARE A SPECIALTY

In Scotland, not only was it considered bad luck to see a hare before going aboard ship (worse luck to find one as a fellow passenger), but fishermen were warned not even to mention the word "rabbit." The Portuguese did not share these beliefs. In the 1400s, Portuguese sailors kept rabbits on their ships as their main source of food.

Hare Today, Gone Tomorrow: Where's Bunnicula?

> *"Just think of it, Harold, if Bunnicula got out, this entire neighborhood could be filled with killer parsnips, blood-thirsty string beans, homicidal heads of lettuce!"*
> —*from* The Celery Stalks at Midnight

Bunnicula has vanished from his cage. Chester's sure the vegetarian vampire rabbit is up to no good. Can you help Chester and Harold find Bunnicula before he gets to all the vegetables in Centerville? You might also find evidence that Bunnicula's been in the neighborhood. See if you can spot the 12 vegetables Bunnicula has attacked. Each one has two small dots—the mark of the vampire!

The solution appears on page 157.

Pencil Pause

How to Draw Bunnicula

Bunnicula's Crossword Puzzle

The solution appears on page 157.

Across

1. ___ a silly question, get a silly answer.

4. A vampire wears a long, black one.

6. Frankenstein's monster was brought to life by _____ of lightning (plural).

10. Chester believes Bunnicula is a _____.

11. Television, for short.

13. What do you want to __ when you grow up?

14. Vampires' pointy teeth.

16. 2, 4, 6 are even numbers. 1, 3, 5 are ___ numbers.

18. Toby and Pete pitch a ___ when they go camping.

19. Nickname for Roger.

21. Abbreviation for "southeast."

22. ___ cubes make drinks colder.

24. _____ Monroe was a famous movie actress.

26. Toby: "Is, too!" Pete: "Is ___!"

28. A type of hawk used for hunting; often perches on its master's wrist.

30. Most stage plays are divided into two or three parts called ____.

33. Means "a lot." Chester is ___ worried about Bunnicula.

34. Between sol and ti.

35. The Hawkeye state; the capital is Des Moines.

38. Nickname for Albert.

39. "Bunnicula" is a name for a vampire rabbit; what name might you give a monster pig?

42. Old-fashioned places to stay when traveling.

43. Microwave or regular, it's the place for cooking.

46. Abbreviation for North Carolina.

47. Looks without blinking. Bunnicula does this with his red eyes.

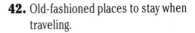

48. Powdery stuff left after a fire (plural).

Down

2. Rescued.

3. People walk; rabbits ___.

5. An insult is a ___-down.

6. An expensive German-made car popular in America.

7. Chester tends to believe everything is a matter of ____ or death.

8. Where vampires supposedly come from.

9. A statement containing a noun or pronoun and a verb.

12. Bunnicula turns these white.

13. Jack-in-the-___.

15. Opposite of chubby.

17. On cold, windy days we sometimes feel a _____ coming under the door.

18. Abbreviation for "Thank goodness it's Friday."

20. Please choose one thing ___ the other.

23. Abbreviation for Colorado.

25. Abbreviation for Los Angeles.

27. A baby cow.

29. Abbreviation for Oregon.

31. Bugs Bunny munches one when he says, "What's up, Doc?"

32. Someone who makes music with his or her voice.

36. Abbreviation for Oklahoma.

37. Plural pronoun, first person.

38. Author of "The Baby-Sitters Club" books is ___ M. Martin.

40. Pete hopes his soccer team ____ enough games to make the playoffs.

41. One twelfth of a foot.

44. Abbreviation for Virginia.

45. Abbreviation for Nebraska.

The "Rabbit-Cadabra!" Magic Trick

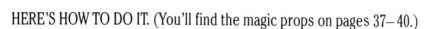

Have you ever seen a magician pull a rabbit out of a hat? Well, you can pull Bunnicula out of yours! Place a carrot in an empty hat—and Bunnicula will magically appear from inside the hat instead.

HERE'S HOW TO DO IT. (You'll find the magic props on pages 37– 40.)

Getting Your Props Ready

To make the props for the "Rabbit-Cadabra!" Magic Trick:

1. Very carefully, cut out the pieces from pages 37– 40 along the **solid black lines.**

2. Fold the HAT CARD along the broken lines so that A meets B. Glue or tape the striped area together (use double-sided tape). Be careful not to get glue in any other area.

3. Fold the HAT CARD along the dotted lines.

The Secret

After you assemble the HAT CARD, you will notice that the folded section forms a pocket—this is the SECRET COMPARTMENT. Gently squeeze the edges of the pocket and they will separate slightly. Now that you know where the SECRET COMPARTMENT is and how to open it, you are ready to start.

Before Performing

Hold the folded HAT CARD so the SECRET COMPARTMENT side is facing the audience. Hold the card as shown in **Fig. A**. Slip the RABBIT CARD under your thumb and hold it securely (**Fig. B**).

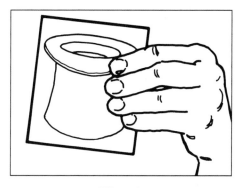

Fig. A

Fig. B

Now You Are Ready to Perform

1. Show the folded-together HAT CARD to the audience. Say something like, "Have you heard about Bunnicula, the vampire rabbit who sucks the juice out of vegetables? Well, I've heard he's hiding somewhere nearby. He might be as near as this hat—although it looks to me as if the hat is empty."

2. With your free hand, fold down the front half of the HAT CARD and show the unfolded card to the audience (**Fig. C**). Say, "Nothing is here." Be careful not to let anyone see the RABBIT CARD.

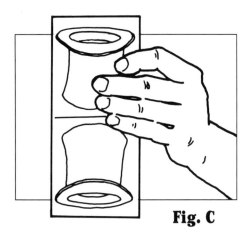

Fig. C

3. Now grasp the bottom of the HAT CARD and fold it back and up so that the RABBIT CARD is wedged between the halves of the HAT CARD (**Fig. D**). You should be holding the HAT CARD in one hand, as shown in **Fig. E**.

Fig. D

Fig. E

4. Squeeze gently at the top edges to open the SECRET COMPARTMENT. Then pick up the CARROT CARD and say, "Maybe he would like some carrots?" Push the CARROT CARD into the SECRET COMPARTMENT (**Fig. F**).

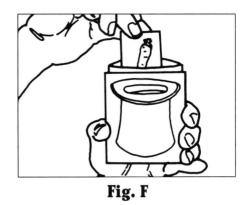

Fig. F

5. Pick up the MAGIC WAND and wave it over the HAT CARD saying, "Bunnicula, Bunnicula, please come out."

6. Lower the front of the HAT CARD toward the audience and say, "There's Bunnicula! And the carrots have turned white!" The RABBIT CARD will now come into view (**Fig. G**). Your audience will think not only that the carrots have made Bunnicula

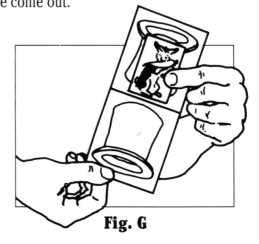

Fig. G

appear, but that he has turned the carrots from orange to white.

7. Turn your hand sideways to show that nothing is hidden on the other side of the HAT CARD.

The "Rabbit-Cadabra!" Magic Trick Props

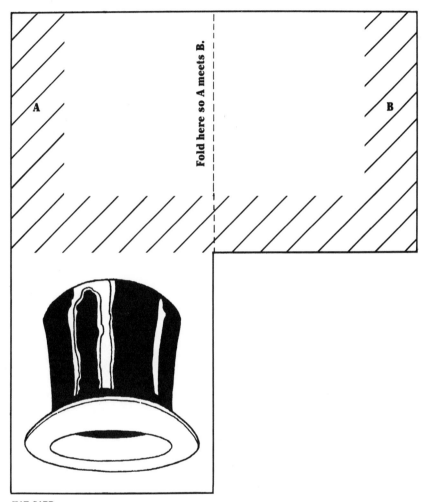

Fold here so A meets B.

A

B

HAT CARD

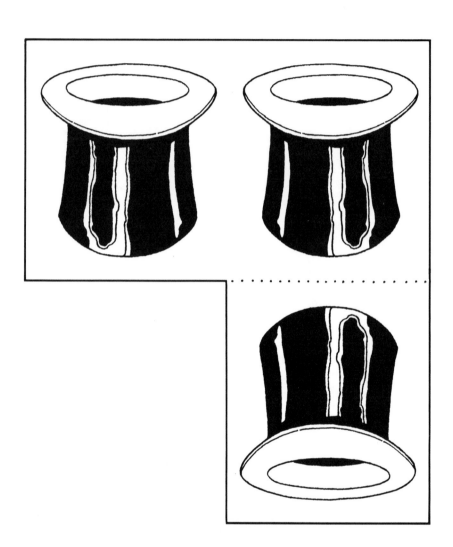

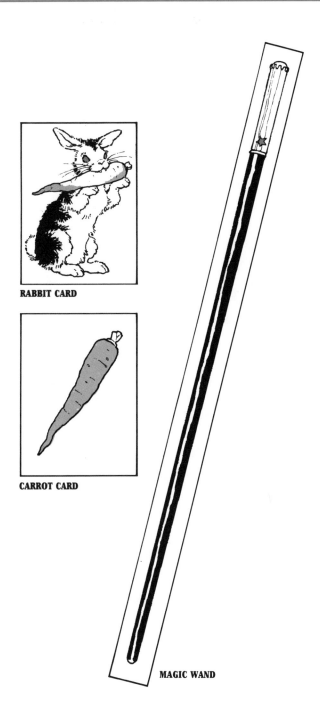

RABBIT CARD

CARROT CARD

MAGIC WAND

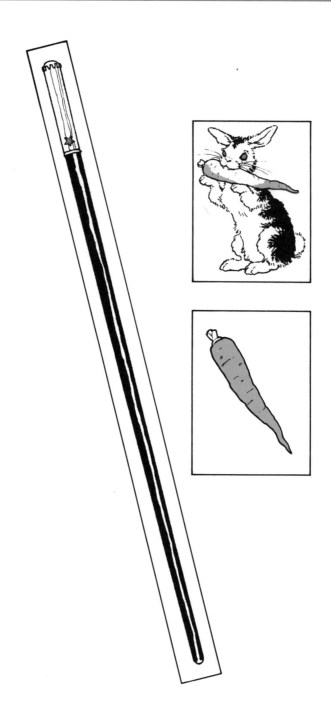

Famous Rabbits

Bugs Bunny

Bugs Bunny is to rabbits what Mickey Mouse is to rodents: a superstar! The wacky "wabbit" made his first appearance in a 1938 Warner Bros. cartoon directed by Ben Hardaway. Ben's nickname was "Bugs," and the unnamed rabbit became known as "Bugs's bunny." In 1940, two now-famous animators, Chuck Jones and Tex Avery, refined Bugs, giving him the looks and personality we've come to associate with the streetwise bunny. His well-known line "What's up, Doc?" was a phrase that had been very popular at Tex's high school. Mel Blanc gave Bugs his Brooklyn-accented voice and continued to be the voice behind the rabbit for almost fifty years!

Bugs was the first cartoon rabbit to win an Oscar —in 1958 for *Knighty-Knight Bugs.* Besides being a movie star, Bugs has appeared in his own TV series, in comic strips, and in comic books.

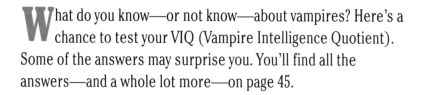

What's Your VIQ?

What do you know—or not know—about vampires? Here's a chance to test your VIQ (Vampire Intelligence Quotient). Some of the answers may surprise you. You'll find all the answers—and a whole lot more—on page 45.

1. Which of the following is *not* the name of a real vampire movie?
    a) *Dracula's Dog*
    b) *Dracula Is Dead and Well and Living in London*
    c) *Dracula's Excellent Adventure*
    d) *Count Downe—Son of Dracula*

2. Who was the author of the book *Dracula*, published in 1897 in England?
    a) James Howe
    b) Bram Stoker
    c) Stephen King
    d) Edgar Allan Poe

3. In the classic 1931 movie *Dracula*, who played the vampire?
    a) Roseanne Arnold
    b) Arnold Schwarzenegger
    c) Boris Karloff
    d) Bela Lugosi

4. On what day was the 1931 movie *Dracula* originally scheduled to have its premiere?

    a) Friday the 13th

    b) Halloween

    c) Valentine's Day

    d) April Fool's Day

5. Which of the following is *not* a vampire myth?

    a) Vampires sleep during the day and stalk their victims at night.

    b) One way to protect yourself from a vampire is to place mistletoe in the doorways and windows of your house.

    c) A vampire cannot see his or her reflection in a mirror.

    d) Vampires can transform themselves into cats.

6. What is *Dark Shadows*?

    a) a vampire rock band

    b) a television soap opera about vampires

    c) a brand of eye makeup preferred by 9 out of 10 vampires

    d) a Transylvanian suburb

7. It is sometimes said that the "real" Dracula was a Transylvanian prince who lived in the 1400s. What was his name?

    a) Count Chocula, also known as "The Vampire with a Sweet Fang"

    b) Vlad Tepes, also known as "Vlad the Impaler"

    c) Erip Mavami, also known as "The Backward Vampire"

    d) Dave, also known as "Jeff"

8. "Dracula" is based on the Hungarian word "dracul." What does "dracul" mean in English?

    a) dentist

    b) vacuum cleaner

    c) devil

    d) person who lives in a castle and uses an answering machine to take telephone calls during daylight hours

9. What is unusual about the way vampires sleep?

    a) They never brush their fangs first.

    b) They wear jammies with feet.

    c) They snore with a Transylvanian accent.

    d) They sleep in their coffins.

10. Which of the following is *not* a way to become a vampire?

    a) be the victim of a vampire

    b) be born with teeth

    c) be the seventh son or daughter of a family with only sons or daughters

    d) watch too much television

Answers to
What's Your VIQ?

1. c   Since the days of silent movies, countless films have been made about vampires. Although such movies have come from every filmmaking country in the world, England has probably produced more than any other single nation. *Dracula's Dog* (1977), *Dracula Is Dead and Well and Living in London* (1975), and *Count Downe— Son of Dracula* (1973) are all British.

2. b   Although he wrote *Dracula* and other books of horror and the supernatural, Bram Stoker wasn't born in Transylvania but in Dublin, Ireland, in 1847. Originally calling it *The Un-dead*, Stoker wrote and edited his book on a recent invention: the typewriter. The book's publication as *Dracula* in 1897 established the title character as the most famous literary vampire ever!

3. d   And Bela Lugosi was the most famous Dracula ever. Hungarian by birth, he possessed an accent that was perfect for the role of the Transylvanian count. Lugosi not only created an image of Dracula that would outlast any other actor's, he became typecast for the rest of his career. When he died in 1956, he was buried in his celebrated black cape—Dracula to the end!

4. *a* The world premiere of *Dracula* was planned for Friday, February 13th, at the Roxy Theatre in New York City. Advertisements, written in dripping red letters, read: I'LL BE ON YOUR NECK FRIDAY THE 13TH—DRACULA. At the last minute, however, the producers, worrying about how their picture was going to do at the box office, decided not to jinx their luck. They opened a day early, on Thursday, February 12th. Producers of the 1992 movie *Bram Stoker's Dracula* were clearly less superstitious. They opened their movie on Friday the 13th of November.

5. *b* It isn't mistletoe that protects you from vampires, it's *garlic*.

If you picked *d*, you made a *myth*take. According to a Japanese legend, vampires can turn themselves into cats, who then sink their fangs into their victims' throats. It should be noted, however, that this legend is the exception to most Asian mythology, which holds cats in high regard.

6. *b* *Dark Shadows* was an enormously popular daytime soap opera that ran on ABC Television from 1966 to 1971. Featuring a vampire-hero named Barnabas Collins, the show also inspired two movies: *House of Dark Shadows* (1970) and *Night of Dark Shadows* (1971). To this day, fans still gather at "Dark Shadows" conventions and watch their favorite episodes on videotape.

7. *b* Vlad Tepes (1431–76) wasn't a vampire. In fact, he was a war hero and ruler of the kingdom of Walachia. However, he was extraordinarily cruel, known for killing enemy soldiers by impaling them on tall wooden poles and leaving them there to die. It is said that after one battle in 1456, he did this to 20,000 men! Vlad Tepes was also called Prince Dracula, because his father was named Dracul.

By the way, did you figure out why Erip Mavami is known as "The Backward Vampire?" Try spelling his name in reverse!

8. *c* "Dracul" means "devil," and "Dracula" means "son of Dracul" or "little devil."

9. *d* Legend has it that vampires, who supposedly have risen from their graves, must return to their coffins—and the soil of their homelands—each night before the rising of the sun. If, like Count Dracula, they travel away from their homeland, they must bring their native soil with them.

10. *d* Watching too much television has been blamed for many ills, but to the best of anyone's knowledge it has yet to turn viewers into vampires. Then again, no one has yet studied the long-range effects of watching those *Dark Shadows* episodes over and over . . . again and again and again.

Harold's Crossword Puzzle

The solution appears on page 158.

Across

1. Describes Harold's haircut or a kind of long-haired rug.

4. Two similar types of dogs are cocker and springer _____.

10. Do re mi fa sol la __ do.

11. A popular kind of music that you talk-sing.

13. A vacation or a stumble.

14. A cat is a feline; a dog is a ___.

16. What Harold did when he was hungry.

18. Dogs' favorite "rest stops" when they're out for a walk.

21. Abbreviation for Tennessee.

22. Masculine pronoun.

23. Toby and Pete followed a trail as they ___ through the woods.

24. Wooden box used for packing and shipping.

25. Opposite of most.

28. We make someone feel at home by putting out the ___ mat.

30. Quiet __ _ mouse.

32. Past tense of light.

34. Howie is this kind of "hot dog" dog.

36. An annoyance to dogs that don't wear the right kind of collar.

37. What a magician pulls a rabbit out of.

Down

1. Abbreviation for Street.

2. Dogs say it by sniffing one another; we say it instead of "hello."

3. An old rabbit might be called a "___ hare."

4. When we cheer for our team, we're showing school ___.

5. When Harold writes, he might use a pencil or _ ___.

6. "That's ___!" Chester cries when he's figured out the answer.

7. A period of time.

8. Dogs and cats and rabbits are born in groups called ___.

9. Toby saves his allowance; Pete likes to ___ his.

12. Howie is Chester's friend ___ _____'_, too.

14. Harold's favorite food—whether it's in cake, ice cream, or candy bars.

15. The dog's is "Harold." The cat's is "Chester." The puppy's is "Howie."

17. A hairy, scary creature, half wild dog and half human.

19. Two important pieces of dog equipment: the collar and ___ _____.

20. The way a chihuahua might say "yes."

26. "It's _____ time!" Chester exclaims when Harold shows up late.

27. These amphibians are similar to frogs, but are warty instead of smooth.

29. All dogs are special, ___ and every one!

31. Please be quiet.

33. Abbreviation for Illinois.

35. A very short laugh.

Pencil Pause

How to Draw Harold

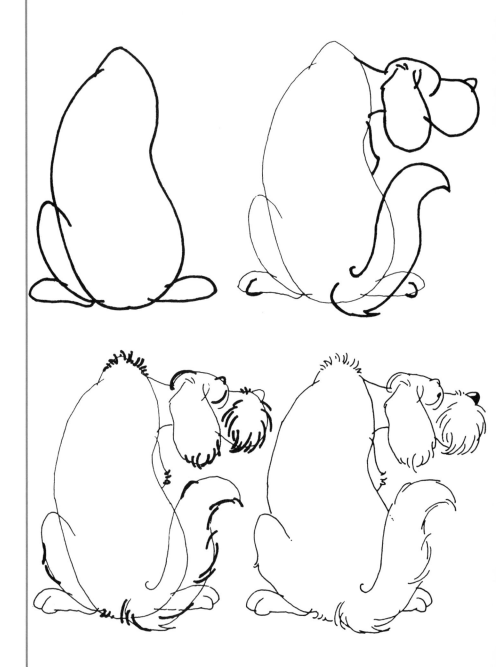

Harold's Magic Hat Puzzle

Each word on the left holds one letter in a magic hat. The clue on the right will help you to fill in the blanks and find the magic letters. After you've pulled all the letters from the hats, put them in the spaces at the bottom to answer one more puzzle: What is **Harold's dream**?

The solutions appear on page 158.

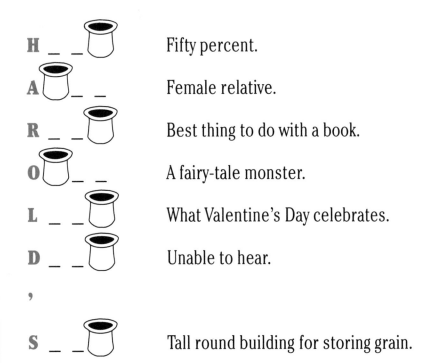

H _ _ ⊔   Fifty percent.

A⊔_ _   Female relative.

R _ _ ⊔   Best thing to do with a book.

O⊔_ _   A fairy-tale monster.

L _ _ ⊔   What Valentine's Day celebrates.

D _ _ ⊔   Unable to hear.

,

S _ _ ⊔   Tall round building for storing grain.

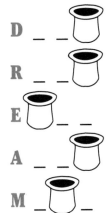

D _ _ ⊔ Opening in a wall; not a window.

R _ _ ⊔ Lawn tool used with leaves.

E ⊔ _ _ Opposite of odd.

A _ _ ⊔ Dull pain.

M _ ⊔ _ Not less.

Harold's Dream:

_ _ _ _ _   _ _ _ _ _ _ _ ! !

Mr. Monroe's Famous Fudge

Mr. Monroe is famous for his fudge. You'll understand why after you've made it yourself. You might want to ask an adult to help you. This fudge will taste delicious whether it's made by two hands or four. And don't forget to let the "hot fudge" get cool before eating it!

> 2 ounces unsweetened chocolate, in squares or
>   liquid packets
> 1/3 cup light corn syrup
> 1/2 cup milk
> 2 cups sugar
> 2 tablespoons butter or margarine
> 1 teaspoon vanilla
> chopped walnuts to taste

Put the chocolate, corn syrup, milk, and sugar in a deep saucepan and cook over low heat. Stir constantly until everything is dissolved completely. Turn the heat up slightly and boil slowly until the chocolate forms a soft ball in cold water. (This part can be tricky. Drop a little bit of the chocolate into a cup of cold water with a spoon, wait a few seconds, then try to form the chocolate into a soft, slightly squishy ball that rolls gently between your fingers. If it falls apart, it's too liquidy, so boil it a little longer. You may need to repeat this test frequently until the chocolate is the right consistency.) Remove the saucepan from the heat. Stir in the butter and vanilla. Let the mixture cool for ten to fifteen minutes. Then beat it with a large spoon, a strong arm, and patience. Beating, by the way, isn't the same as stirring; beating means to stir vigorously, like you mean it! The fudge has been beaten long enough when you can feel it thickening and the surface loses some of its shine and begins to look a little dull.

Stir in the nuts. Pour the fudge into a lightly greased pie plate or pan. Let the mixture sit until it's cooled completely. Cut the fudge into pieces with a sharp, moist knife. Pour yourself some milk and dig in.

Harold's Brain Benders

Harold says:

"I think of the Monroe family as pretty ordinary. But every once in a while, I observe something I just can't explain. When that happens, I find Chester. I don't know how he does it, but he always manages to figure out the most puzzling situation. See if *you* can figure out what was happening in each of the following three cases."

The answers appear on page 159.

Brain Bender #1: "The Stamp in the Cocoa"

One day, I overheard Toby telling his friend Ben, "Boy, was I clever last night. I was working on my stamp collection in the kitchen when Pete came in and asked if I had an Elvis stamp. Well, you know Pete. If I'd told him I had, he would have grabbed it. So you know what I did? I dropped it in my cocoa!"

That didn't sound very clever to me. When I told Chester about it, he said, "I was in the kitchen when this happened, Harold, and Toby was very clever. As soon as Pete left the room, Toby took the stamp out of the cocoa, and it was just fine."

"But how can that be?" I asked. *Do you know?*

Brain Bender #2: "Twins?"

One summer afternoon, the Monroes were sitting in the backyard having lunch with their guests: two men who looked exactly alike.

"Boy," I said to Chester, "it's really confusing telling twins apart."

"They're not twins," Chester told me.

"Stop pulling my leg."

"I'm not pulling your leg. They were born on the same day in the same year. They have the same mother and father, and they look alike. But I can promise you, Harold, they are not twins."

"How can that be?" *Do you know?*

Brain Bender #3: "It Isn't Fair!"

My late-afternoon nap was rudely interrupted by the return of Toby and Pete from a day at the amusement park.

"It isn't fair!" Toby shouted. "We agreed to split our prizes even-Steven!"

"We *are* splitting them," said Pete. "You get one candy bar. I get the other."

"Yeah, and I know which one I get," Toby said with a frown.

I looked at the two candy bars Pete held in his hands. One was your basic sliver of chocolate in a wrapper, what I call a two-gulper. The other was a huge one-pounder—a week's supply, at least. No wonder Toby was upset.

"Okay," Pete said, "I'll tell you what we'll do. I'll take two pieces of paper. On one I'll write 'big' and on the other I'll write 'little.' Whichever one you draw, that's the candy bar you get. Fair enough?"

When Pete left the room to get some paper, Toby looked at me and winked. "There's no way Pete is going to let me have that big candy bar," he said. "I'm sure he's going to write 'little' on both pieces of paper. But two can play at that game. I'll end up with that big bar of chocolate yet, Harold, just you wait and see."

I couldn't figure out how he was going to do it, but Chester, who had been watching the whole thing from his favorite armchair, had it all figured out.

How was Toby going to get the big candy bar? *Do you know?*

Write On!

The Case of the . . .

In *Howliday Inn*, Harold becomes a detective when Chester disappears. Imagine that *you* are a detective. Fill in the following information, and then write a story based on it using pages 62–63.

Your detective name: _____

The name of your detective agency:

_____

The kinds of cases you specialize in: _____

_____

_____

How long you've been in business: _____

Your best case (biggest triumph): _____

_____

_____

Your worst case (greatest humiliation): _____

_____

_____

The day this story begins: _____

The person who comes to your office: _____

_____

The mystery she or he presents to you: _____

_____

_____

What she or he wants you to do or to find: _____

_____

_____

Now write a story about how you solve the case!

_____

_____

_____

_____

_____

_____

_____

_____

_____

_____

_____

_____

_____

_____

_____

_____

_____

_____

_____

_____

_____

_____

_____

_____

_____

_____

_____

_____

You Lucky Dog!

Superstitions About Dogs

🐾 In Ireland, it is considered unlucky for a woman to kiss a dog on her wedding day.

🐾 The Dog societies of the Crow and Hidatsa Indians of the Great Plains reflect the belief that the dog is a symbol of bravery.

🐾 A dog's howling has often been seen as an omen of death. In Tennessee, a dog howling for three nights in a row was a sure sign that death would follow, while in Texas certain death was predicted by a dog howling while lying on its back. In some parts of England, to quiet a howling dog—and thereby avoid death—people would take off their left shoes and turn them upside down.

And why did a howling dog predict death? Because it was believed that dogs could see the spirit of Death, which was invisible to humans.

 *"He followed me home. Can I keep him?"* Many superstitions tell us that it is good luck to be followed by a dog. In some southern states, you would be advised *always* to keep any strange dog that followed you home. In Maryland, to be followed by a *yellow* dog was especially good luck.

 In English tradition, not only is there a man in the moon, but a dog as well. Various American Indian tribes have their own "dogs in the moon." The Shawnees, for instance, see an old woman with her little dog beside her. The Central Inuit see a sled drawn by a dog. And the Ojibwa behold a man with a dog in his lap.

 Clay statues of harnessed dogs have been found in ancient Chinese tombs, because it was believed that dogs would act as guides for the deceased on the journey into the hereafter.

Did You Know . . .
About Rabbits?

Rabbits have been around for over 30 million years.

Rabbits originated in northwest Africa, Spain, and Portugal. All the rabbits in the United States are descendents of these wild European rabbits.

Never hold a rabbit by the ears! Forget all those pictures you've seen of magicians pulling rabbits out of hats. The proper way to hold a rabbit is by the loose skin at the back of its neck, while you support its hindquarters with your other hand.

Did you ever hear a rabbit scream? That's what wild rabbits sometimes do when they've been caught. The loud, piercing scream surprises the attacker so much that it drops the rabbit, which runs away free. The scream also acts as a warning to other rabbits in the area.

Famous Rabbits

The Easter Bunny

The origins of the Easter Bunny are unknown. What is known is that in myths and folklore the world over, the rabbit—or, more correctly, the hare—has long been associated with the moon. The date of the Easter holiday, decided on in the year 325 A.D., is also associated with the moon. Easter is a Spring holiday, and Spring is seen as the dawn of the year. Likewise, the hare has been a symbol of dawn and birth. The word "Easter" comes from Eostre, the name of an Anglo-Saxon goddess of the dawn. Eostre's favorite animal was said to be the hare. One legend has it that she created the first hare from a bird. The hare was so thankful that each year it laid brightly colored eggs in Eostre's honor.

Over time, these various associations and legends have combined to give us the character of the egg-carrying bunny, a modern symbol of Easter throughout much of the world.

Mixed-Up Animals

Howie is a young dog, or puppy. Sometimes, he doesn't understand things and gets all mixed up. The young animals below are mixed up, too. Their names are scrambled. Unscramble each name, and write it in the blanks to the right of each scrambled name.

Then try to solve the puzzle on page 69.

The solution appears on page 159.

A. NUBYN   _ _ _ _ _

B. BLAM   _ _ _ _

C. WNAF   _ _ _ _

D. CCKIH   _ _ _ _ _

E. TAPLEDO   _ _ _ _ _ _ _

F. LETOW   _ _ _ _ _

G. IKD   _ _ _

H. UPYPP   _ _ _ _ _

I. UCB   _ _ _

J. NTKEIT   _ _ _ _ _ _

K. PILCERRAATL   _ _ _ _ _ _ _ _ _ _ _

68

L. LINSGOG   _ _ _ _ _ _ _

M. FLAC   _ _ _ _

N. LUDKNGIC   _ _ _ _ _ _ _ _

O. GLEEAT   _ _ _ _ _ _

P. ALOF   _ _ _ _

Q. NTYGCE   _ _ _ _ _ _

Using the unscrambled names of the different kinds of young animals, match each one to its parent by writing the letter in the blank. *The solution appears on page 159.*

1. Dog   _____   **9.** Lion   _____

2. Cat   _____   **10.** Swan   _____

3. Owl   _____   **11.** Goat   _____

4. Rabbit   _____   **12.** Butterfly   _____

5. Goose   _____   **13.** Eagle   _____

6. Hen   _____   **14.** Sheep   _____

7. Frog   _____   **15.** Duck   _____

8. Horse   _____   **16.** Cow   _____

17. Deer   _____

Word Find

Young Animals

You like to play; young animals do, too. So the animals listed below are hiding among the letters on the next page. Can you find them? Remember that the words may run from left to right or from right to left, from top to bottom or from bottom to top, or on a diagonal in either direction. But whichever way they go, the letters always follow a straight line.

The solution appears on page 159.

BUNNY	DUCKLING	KITTEN
CALF	EAGLET	LAMB
CATERPILLAR	FAWN	OWLET
CHICK	FOAL	PUPPY
CUB	GOSLING	TADPOLE
CYGNET	KID	

```
H  C  F  A  O  L  I  Y  B  A  R  W
B  E  A  G  L  E  T  N  F  L  A  C
O  G  E  T  E  N  O  N  T  A  O  C
C  O  O  L  E  K  X  U  A  O  M  A
H  S  Z  T  I  R  A  B  D  F  I  L
I  L  T  T  K  L  P  U  P  P  Y  M
C  I  T  S  I  Q  R  I  O  A  Z  O
K  N  O  B  D  U  C  K  L  I  N  G
I  G  M  U  U  E  B  T  E  L  W  O
T  E  N  G  Y  C  F  R  A  D  A  P
C  A  T  R  A  R  C  M  N  O  F  R
Y  S  G  K  N  T  B  F  A  R  M  O
```

Did You Know . . .
About Halloween?

Halloween probably started over 2,000 years ago with a Celtic festival called Samhain. The Celts, a European people who lived in France and the British Isles, believed that dead spirits came back to earth on the night of October 31. During the festival of Samhain, they built fires and wore costumes in order to scare away the ghosts.

In the early 600s, many Celts had become Christians and Samhain was combined with the Christian holiday of All Hallows' Day. The night before All Hallows' Day was called All Hallows' Even. In time, "All Hallows' Even" became known as "Halloween."

AH-CHOO! In Wales, people were afraid to sneeze on Halloween. Why? On that night, it was believed the devil was on the prowl. It was also believed that sneezing shot the soul out of one's body for a split second, just long enough for the devil to snatch it away. By quickly saying "God bless you" to a sneezer, one could get in the devil's way and save a soul!

In England and Ireland, where the custom began, jack-o'-lanterns were first made out of turnips.

Trick or treating started in Ireland, where poor people went from house to house asking for money or food. Saying the words "trick or treat" did not become part of Halloween tradition until the 1940s in the United States.

A witch riding on a flying broomstick is a familiar image of Halloween, even though no one has actually seen a witch—or a broomstick—fly. In the late fifteenth century, a manual for witch hunters was written. It was called *Malleus Maleficarum*, and it provided a long list of signs by which to recognize witches. One identifying sign was the flying broom. It is doubtful that the authors based this "observation" on anything other than their overheated imaginations, but the flying broom has been part of witch mythology ever since.

What Are You Afraid Of?

Halloween is a time for being scared. But some people are scared of something *all* the time. They have a condition that is called a phobia. Here are some phobias that must be even worse at Halloween!

bogyphobia   fear of demons and goblins

dromophobia   fear of crossing streets (a real problem for trick-or-treaters!)

lygophobia   fear of the dark

taphephobia   fear of cemeteries or being buried alive

We mere mortals aren't the only ones to be afraid, however. If you were a vampire, you'd have all of these phobias:

aichurophobia fear of being touched by pointed objects
aquaphobia fear of water
phengophobia fear of daylight
spectrophobia fear of looking in the mirror
staurophobia fear of crosses and crucifixes

You might learn to live with these fears. But if you were a vampire with **hematophobia**, you'd be in big trouble. What is hematophobia? Fear of the sight of blood!

A-maze-ing!

The House of Dr.E.A.D.

> *"Listen, Harold," Chester said, "the woods are full of spirits."*
>
> *"What woods?"*
>
> *"Any woods. They're dark places, Harold, harboring evil creatures who prey on the innocent."*
>
> *"Do the Boy Scouts know about this?" I asked.*
>
> *—from* Nighty-Nightmare

You're lost in the woods. The fog is getting thicker. You've got to get home before you fall into the clutches of the mad scientist Dr. Emil Alphonse Diabolicus. If he doesn't get you, his crazed housekeeper, Erda, just might! Watch out—don't fall into a pit or wander into a cage. And remember: If you end up at the House of Dr.E.A.D., you're in for a long, *long* visit.

What's that howling? Quick! Hurry home!!

The solution appears on page 160.

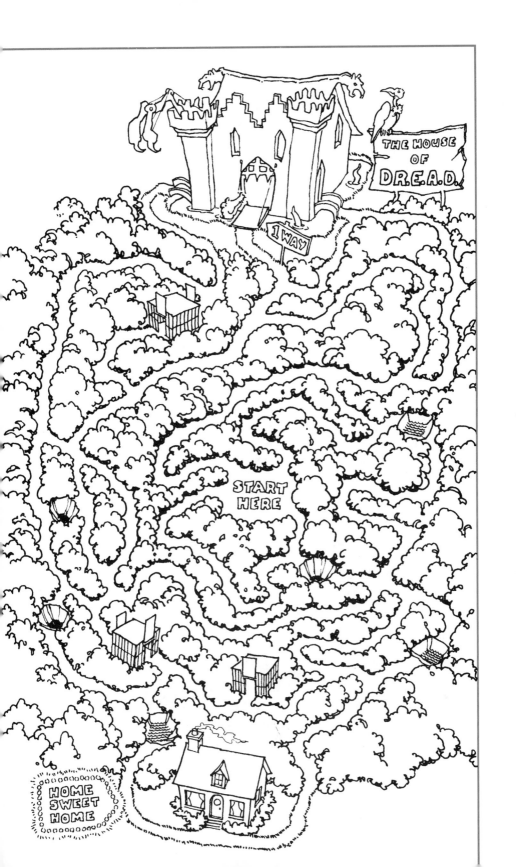

Wacky Words!

Wacky Words! is a game that's fun for one person, two people, or the whole gang. If you're playing it alone, fill in the list on the next page with whatever words come to mind. Don't turn the page until you've completed the entire list. *Then* turn the page and fill in the blanks in the story, using the words you've listed here.

If you're playing with others, go directly to page 80. Announce the type of word called for under each blank. Each of the other players takes a turn providing a word that fits. Don't read any of the story aloud until all the blanks are filled in. Then read it from beginning to end—and just try to keep from laughing! The wackiest, funniest, and most descriptive words will give you the wildest, craziest stories!

Vampire Rap

1. ADJECTIVE

2. PLURAL NOUN

3. VERB

4. VERB

5. VERB

6. BODY PART

7. COLOR

8. NOUN

9. NOUN

10. NOUN

11. LIQUID

12. ADJECTIVE

13. ADJECTIVE

14. ADJECTIVE

15. VERB

16. VERB

17. PLURAL NOUN

79

Wacky Words!

Vampire Rap

Well, did you ever see a vampire out in the night?

He's kind of _____ ; he'll give you a fright!
(1. adjective)

Watch out for his _____ , if you know what I
(2. plural noun)

    mean,

'Cause they can _____ and they can
(3. verb)

    _____ and everythin' in between.
    (4. verb)

If a vampire catches you, you're in for a surprise:

He'll _____ you on the _____ , and hold
(5. verb)   *(6. body part)*

    you with his eyes.

Then he'll turn you _____ and laugh right in your
(7. color)

    face,

Sayin', "You're a _____ now, and that's no
(8. noun)

    disgrace!"

So if you see a vampire comin', here's what you do:

Hold up a _____ till he runs away from you,
(9. noun)

Take a sharp _____ and drive it through his heart,
(10. noun)

Splash him with some _____ and watch him fall
(11. liquid)

   apart!

I'm talkin' vampires: _____ , _____ ,
(12. adjective)   *(13. adjective)*

_____ vampires!
(14. adjective)

Vampires who _____ and vampires who bite!
(15. verb)

Vampires who love to _____ you and give you a
(16. verb)

   fright!

Vampires in the mornin' and vampires at night!

V-A-M-P-I-R-E-S, that spells _____ !
(17. plural noun)

Pencil Pause

Design Your Own Halloween Costume

Draw the best Halloween costume that you can imagine. Make it the scariest, funniest, weirdest, or wildest one ever!

Now draw a mask to go with it.

Word Find

Creepy Creatures

The creepy creatures listed below are lurking in this Word Find. See if you can spot them among all the letters on the next page. The words may run from left to right or from right to left, from top to bottom or from bottom to top, or on a diagonal in either direction. But whichever way they go, the letters always follow a straight line.

Watch out: Two of these creatures are lurking in pairs! If you can't find them, look at the bottom of page 86 and you'll see which ones they are. Then try looking for them again.

The solution appears on page 160.

BIGFOOT	PHANTOM
DRACULA	SERPENT
FRANKENSTEIN	SKELETON
GHOST	THE THING
GHOUL	TROLL
GOBLIN	VAMPIRE
GODZILLA	WEREWOLF
IMP	WITCH
KING KONG	YETI
MONSTER	ZOMBIE
OGRE	

```
N Y C T E O V T P O L F T I G
I I E H O H A B S Y L Z O N O
L T E E C I M P R O L L O N D
B Y E T I G P T W A H K F E Z
O S I H S H I E M N G G G B I
G W X I A N R Y Z N A C I A L
A R T N Y E E N I S L M B R L
L F N G W L O K L A U S P E A
B B E A L T B L N I C H H T E
S O P O E M O N S A A X A S I
A I R L O R T O O N R E N N B
I T E Z T Z O G R E D F T O M
M K S O O L U O H G A B O M O
S V U E Z O M B I E L K M O Z
```

Howie's Howlers

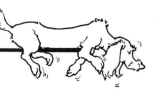

Where do phantoms go to work?

The ghost office.

What kind of music do mummies like best?

Wrap music.

What kind of music do ghosts like best?

Sheet music.

How does a French skeleton say hello?

Bone jour.

What did the little monster's aunt say after seeing her for the first time in a year?

"My, you gruesome!"

Clue for CREEPY CREATURES WORD FIND:

Did you find 2 *trolls* and 2 *zombies*?

How did the monster feel after Dr. Frankenstein cloned him?

Beside himself.

What did the invitation to the Reincarnation Party say?

"Come as you were."

Why didn't the zombie go dancing?

She was dead on her feet.

Why did the little monster eat the tight-rope walkers?

Her mother told her always to eat a well-balanced diet.

Why did the monster send his soup back?

There was only one fly in it.

Itchy Witchy

Itchy Witchy is another name for Inky Pinky, a game in which the first player gives a clear, short definition and the second player translates that definition into two words that rhyme. If each word in the answer has one syllable, the first player says, "Itch Witch." If each word has two syllables, it's an "Itchy Witchy." Here are two examples of an Itch Witch:

> *Definition*: undressed rabbit
> *Answer*: bare hare

> *Definition*: overweight feline
> *Answer*: fat cat

Now that you've got the idea, see how you do on the Halloween-related words on the next page. Then make up your own. Whether you call it Itchy Witchy or Inky Pinky, it's a lot of fun—and it's a great game to play in the car!

The answers appear on page 161.

Itch Witch

1. head apparel for flying mammal

_____   _____

2. invisible bread browned on both sides

_____   _____

3. creature dinner

_____   _____

4. unpolished head bone

_____   _____

5. place in house for witches to keep their special modes of transportation

_____   _____

6. the job of making a face covering

_____   _____

7. fear of being attacked by a vampire

_____   _____

8. peculiar facial hair

_____   _____

9. work implement used by evil creature

_____   _____

10. wealthy broom-rider

_____   _____

Itchy Witchy

1. frightening spirit

_____   _____

2. even demon

_____   _____

3. horrible tale

_____   _____

4. skeleton liar

_____   _____

5. someone who makes others tremble

_____   _____

6. ghostly barnyard fowl

_____   _____

7. broom-rider's treasures

_____   _____

8. a way to hold a stick of burning wax

_____   _____

9. beastly instructor

_____   _____

10. autumn fruit drink made from eight-legged insects

_____   _____

Famous Rabbits

Brer Rabbit

Brer Rabbit was made famous when Joel Chandler Harris published stories about him in the book *Uncle Remus: His Songs and Sayings* in 1880. Harris had learned about this character of African folklore from the black slaves who worked on the plantation where he was a printer's apprentice as a teenager. Mischievous, clever, and lovable, Brer Rabbit was, in Harris's words, "the weakest and most harmless of all animals, but victorious in contests with the bear, the wolf, and the fox." Chandler created the imaginary character of an old former slave, Uncle Remus, to tell the stories of Brer Rabbit. There were ten Uncle Remus books altogether, many of which are still in print.

The Uncle Remus stories were the basis of a 1946 Disney movie, *Song of the South*, which featured the Academy Award-winning song "Zip a Dee Do Dah" and used a mix of live action and animation 42 years before *Who Framed Roger Rabbit.*

Why Do We Say . . .

> Off the slippery roof I tumbled, holding Chester tightly by the tail. Together we landed in a jumble right in front of the door to the bungalow. Max and Georgette turned to discover us lying in a puddle at their doorstep.
> "Look, Max," Georgette said, "it's rainin' cats and dogs."
>
> —*from* Howliday Inn

It's raining cats and dogs.

No one knows for sure how this expression got its start. One possibility is that in ancient Norse mythology, cats were symbols of rainstorms and dogs were symbols of the wind. In many different cultures, cats have been associated with the rain and have been thought to influence the weather. Another thought is that thunder and rain suggest a noisy dog-and-cat fight.

A cat has nine lives.

This expression goes back to ancient times and is no doubt based on the fact that a cat's body is so agile and flexible that the cat is able to survive scrapes that would kill most other animals. The earliest known reference is from a Hindu fable called "The Greedy and Ambitious Cat," dating back to 300 B.C.: "It has been the providence of nature to give this creature nine lives instead of one."

Let the cat out of the bag.

Letting the cat out of the bag means giving away a secret. How did this curious phrase get its start? Before supermarkets, people shopped for their food at farmers' markets. An expensive purchase—and a highly prized one for holidays—was a suckling pig. Sometimes farmers pulled a fast one on unsuspecting customers by substituting a worthless cat for the valuable pig. The customer wouldn't find out she'd been tricked until she got home and "let the cat out of the bag."

Curiosity killed the cat.

This expression started out in the 1500s as "care killed the cat." "Care," in this case, meant "worry," and the idea was that too much worrying was enough to kill anyone—even a cat, with all its nine lives. At some point, "care" changed to "curiosity." With the word change, the meaning changed as well.

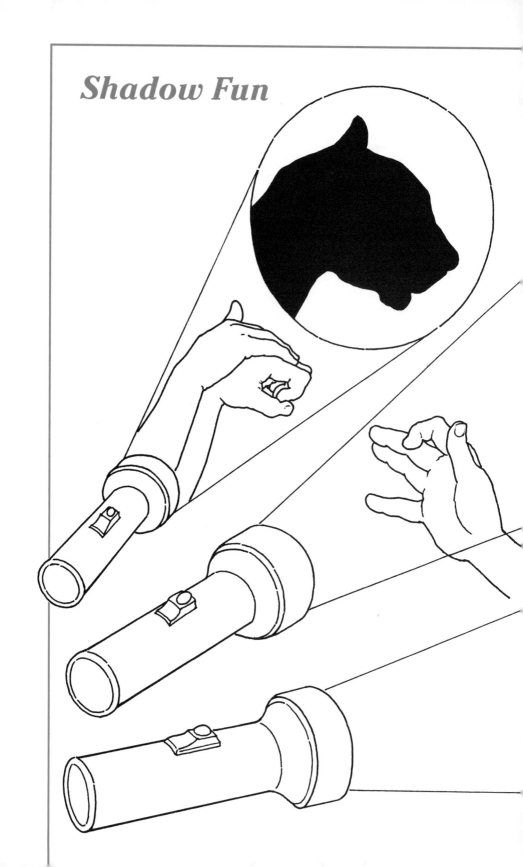

Shadow Fun

Chester's Crossword Puzzle

¹		■	²	³	■		⁴		⁵			⁶	
	■	⁷			⁸		■			■			■
⁹	¹⁰									¹¹	¹²		
¹³			■		■		■		¹⁴				■
	■	¹⁵	¹⁶		■	¹⁷	¹⁸	■	¹⁹			²⁰	²¹
■		²²		²³							²⁴		
²⁵	²⁶					■			■				■
²⁷					■	²⁸		²⁹		³⁰			³¹
³²				■	³³			■		■		³⁴	
	■	³⁵					■	³⁶					■

The solution appears on page 161.

Across

1. Howie calls Chester "Pop" as a nickname for father. He might also say "___."

2. Oppposite of "from."

4. In the Monroe family, Toby is Pete's younger _____.

7. How the word "dog" might be pronounced with a Southern drawl. Also a character in *Nighty-Nightmare*.

9. Famous mystery solver.

13. A very young child.

14. Cats can cause mischief, but they usually don't mean any ____.

15. Another way of saying "Huh? What?"

17. Abbreviation for South Dakota.

20. Former. For example, a former prisoner is an __-convict.

96

22. It's said that _____ killed the cat.

24. Abbreviation for New York.

25. Cats love the smell of this plant. Their toys are often filled with it.

27. To line things up right next to one another.

29. Chester takes this kind of little snooze many times during the day.

32. A cat has nine _____.

33. Sick.

34. Abbreviation for railroad or rural route.

35. When a cat is very alert, it sits straight-backed or _____.

36. Chester was so scared, he felt as if _____ one of his hairs was on end.

Down

1. Macaroni and spaghetti are types of _____.

2. Black sticky material used on roads.

3. Who says "Hoo"?

4. Two-wheeler.

5. When Chester sees trouble ahead, he says, "__-__."

6. 9 across says, "_____, my dear Watson." (Also a type of school.)

7. Another word for mystery solver. Chester is one; so is 9 across.

8. To talk about people behind their backs.

10. Add two more and this is what Santa says.

11. Chester thinks Harold is ___ because he sleeps so much.

12. ___ and Mrs. Monroe.

16. The feeling that tells us it's time to eat.

18. Opposite of "don't."

19. Cats often go around in a _____ before settling down in one spot.

21. The last two before Z.

23. Wash away soap with water.

25. When we want to speak to someone far away, we ____ them on the phone.

26. Former world heavyweight boxing champion Muhammad ____.

28. Cats often squeeze themselves to ___ into the smallest places.

30. Cats bathe so thoroughly they even lick in between each ____.

31. Abbreviation for Puerto Rico.

97

Write On!

Books, Books, Books!

> *"Why aren't you going crazy like everybody else?" I demanded. "What's your secret?"*
>
> *Chester's smile grew more knowing. "Books," he said, with a nod to the one in front of him, "are not only windows to the world, dear Harold, they are pathways to inner peace."*
>
> *I shook my head. "I've tried books," I said. "Fifteen minutes and all I ended up with was cardboard breath."*
>
> —*from* Return to Howliday Inn

Chester is a big reader. So is Toby, whose special treat is to stay up late on Friday nights to read. How do you feel about reading?

I love / like / don't like reading because: _____

_____

My all-time favorite book is: _____

_____

The funniest book I ever read is: _____

_____

_____

The saddest book I ever read is: _____

_____

A book I will never forget is: _____

_____

A book that made me really angry is: _____

_____

My favorite character(s) from a book is/are: _____

_____

The names of the last 3 books I read are: _____

_____

_____

_____

The names of 3 books I want to read are: _____

_____

_____

_____

If I were a writer, I'd write books about: _____

_____

_____

Famous Rabbits

Peter Rabbit

Peter Rabbit is one of the most enduring of all animal characters in literature. Created by a young Englishwoman named Beatrix Potter in 1893, Peter first appeared in a letter written to Noel Moore, the five-year-old son of Beatrix's former governess. Noel was sick in bed with rheumatic fever when seventeen-year-old Beatrix wrote and illustrated the story of Peter Rabbit to entertain him. This was the first of many illustrated letters she would write to children and later turn into books. Peter Rabbit was named after Beatrix Potter's own pet rabbit, who was called Peter Piper. He was not only the main character of that first letter but of the first book, *The Tale of Peter Rabbit*, which was published in 1902 to immediate success.

Another popular rabbit, Peter's cousin Benjamin Bunny, was named for another of Beatrix's pet rabbits. Over the years, she kept many unusual pets, including hedgehogs and bats. *The Tale of Benjamin Bunny* was published in 1904.

Did You Know . . .
About Rabbits & Hares?

We often use the two words to mean the same thing, but a "rabbit" is not the same as a "hare," although the two animals are related. *Hare* are some differences:

Rabbits	Hares
• Small body and short ears	• Large body and long ears
• Color of fur stays the same year round	• Color of fur changes with the seasons
• Runs and scampers	• Hops and leaps
• Lives in groups	• Lives alone
• Lives underground	• Lives above ground
• Babies are born without fur	• Babies are born with fur
• Newborn babies cannot see, hear, or walk	• Newborn babies can see and hop almost immediately

Scrambled Squares

V-V-V-Vampires?!

Legend tells us that a vampire's victim becomes a vampire as well. What happens to Bunnicula's victims? To find out, copy each drawing below into the matching numbered box on the opposite page. And then watch out for v-v-v-v...

The solution appears on page 162.

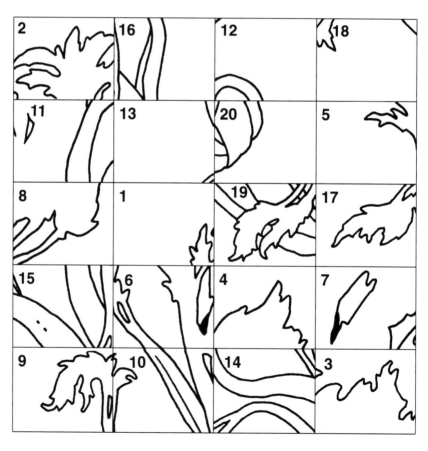

1	2	3	4
5	6	7	8
9	10	11	12
13	14	15	16
17	18	19	20

Write On!

Opening Lines

Here are the real opening sentences of ten Bunnicula books. See if you can tell which book each sentence belongs to.

Then pick one sentence and write your own story on pages 106–107, using it as an opening line. Don't worry about making your story similar to the book it comes from. Just let it spark your own imagination and have fun!

The answers appear on page 162.

1. All day long the sky had been crawling with clouds as mean and restless as ghosts on the prowl. ____

2. It was not a dark and stormy night. ____

3. Looking back on it now, I doubt that there was any way I could have imagined what lay ahead. ____

4. It was Christmas Eve at the Monroes' house. ____

5. I shall never forget the first time I laid these now tired old eyes on our visitor. ____

6. Friday nights are special at our house. ___

7. It began on the bottom of a canoe in the middle of Boggy Lake, some sixty miles from home and fifty yards from solid ground. ___

8. Toby's birthday was here at last. ___

9. It was the third straight day of rain. ___

10. It had been a long time since I'd seen Toby so excited—and all because The Amazing Karlovsky was coming to town. ___

A. *Bunnicula: A Rabbit -Tale of Mystery*
B. *The Celery Stalks at Midnight*
C. *Creepy-Crawly Birthday*
D. *The Fright Before Christmas*
E. *Hot Fudge*
F. *Howliday Inn*
G. *Nighty-Nightmare*
H. *Rabbit-Cadabra!*
I. *Return to Howliday Inn*
J. *Scared Silly: A Halloween Treat*

Howie's Howlers

Why do vampires enjoy family reunions?
  Because they love to attack necks-of-kin.

How did the vampire start his letter?
  Tomb it may concern.

What kind of boats do vampires like best?
  Blood vessels.

Why are vampires easily fooled?
  Because they're all suckers.

Why does a vampire use mouthwash?
  Bat breath.

What position does Dracula play for the Transylvanian Terrors hockey team?

Ghoulie.

What is a vampire's least favorite kind of meat?

Stake.

What are a vampire's favorite kind of beans?

Human beans.

What did the vampire's victim say when asked how he was feeling?

"Oh, I'm all white."

What is a vampire's favorite dessert?

I scream.

Why did the vampires have to call off their softball game?

   The bats flew away.

Why did the vampire attack the hare instead of the tortoise?

   She was in the mood for a quick bite.

Why do vampires think of themselves as artists?

   Because they draw blood.

Where do vampires go to work?

   The Vampire State Building.

What did the vampire get after biting Sleeping Beauty on the neck?

   Tired blood.

Make Up the Name
of a Vampire . . .

Rock band: _____

Amusement-park ride: _____

Sports team: _____

Board game: _____

Dance craze: _____

Dessert: _____

TV show: _____

Planet: _____

Toy: _____

Hit song: _____

Famous Rabbits

Bunnicula

Bunnicula, the vampire rabbit, got his start in the mind of James Howe in the mid-1970s. He and his late wife, Deborah, loved horror movies—especially versions of the Dracula story—and often found them as amusing as they were scary. Although he doesn't know for sure how Bunnicula popped, or hopped, into his imagination, James guesses he may have asked himself, "What creature would make the least likely—and funniest—vampire?" A rabbit came to mind, and Bunnicula was born.

It wasn't until 1977, however, that Deborah's mother pointed out that Bunnicula would make a good character in a children's book. Neither James nor Deborah knew much about children's books other than the ones they themselves had read as children, but they both enjoyed writing. They sat down at once to begin work on what they imagined would be little more than a pleasurable way to pass the time.

Bunnicula: A Rabbit-Tale of Mystery was published in 1979. The book was an immediate hit with readers and led James, who had never planned on becoming a children's author, to write several sequels as well as to create a picture-book series featuring the fang-toothed bunny. Through it all, Bunnicula has remained true to himself—silent, vegetable loving, and as mysterious as ever.

Write On!

If I Were a . . .

All the Bunnicula books are written by Harold, a dog, about his family, the Monroes. Write a story about your family as if it were told by your pet. If you don't have a pet, tell the story from the point of view of something else: a stuffed animal, perhaps, or your TV set or car. Imagine how your family—and you—appear to your made-up storyteller.

_____

_____

_____

_____

_____

_____

_____

_____

_____

_____

Howie's Crossword Puzzle

A s you probably know, Howie loves puns. Puns are jokes that are funny because the words involved have more than one meaning. Each answer in this crossword puzzle is a word with more than one meaning. Therefore, *two* clues are provided for every answer.

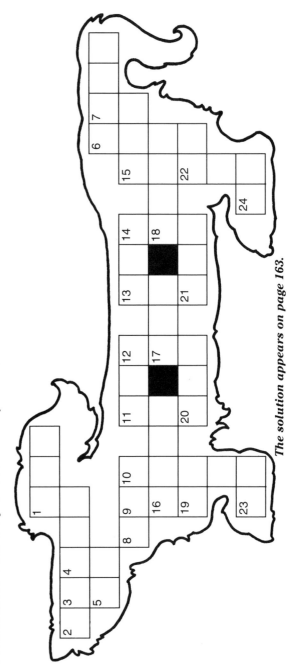

The solution appears on page 163.

Across

1. Howie's name for Chester; the sound a balloon makes when it explodes.

2. What Howie does when the weather's hot; clothing for the legs.

5. Abbreviation for Missouri; nickname for Maureen.

6. A duck's mouth; William's nickname.

8. What Howie says before "Wow"; what an actor takes at a curtain call.

11. Hearing organ; an ___ of corn.

13. Piece of baseball equipment; furry cave-dwelling mammal.

15. Japanese money; strong desire, as in "I have a ___ for ice cream!"

16. Opposite of up; material parkas are stuffed with.

17. Highest card in the deck; get an "A."

18. Oblong, egg-shaped; a running or racing track.

19. To perform an action; first and eighth notes of the musical scale.

20. Dull, almost dark; pessimistic: a ___ view of things.

21. Go for a ___ in the pool; have some potato chips and ___.

22. Abbreviation for "right"; abbreviation for "round trip."

23. You and me together; abbreviation for United States.

24. We are, she ___; abbreviation for "island."

Down

1. Abbreviation for "post script"; abbreviation for "public school."

3. We are, I ___; afternoon = P.M., morning = ___.

4. Negative answer; abbreviation for "north."

6. Hit hard; something you wear around your waist.

7. Opposite of out; abbreviation for Indiana.

9. Strange; opposite of even.

10. A place with a lot of trees; golf clubs, not the irons.

11. Finish; football position: tight ___.

12. Computer abbreviation: "random-access memory"; male sheep.

13. Piece of furniture for sleeping; place for flowers in a garden.

14. Spinning toy; opposite of bottom.

15. Strands of fiber used in knitting; tall tales.

How to Draw Howie

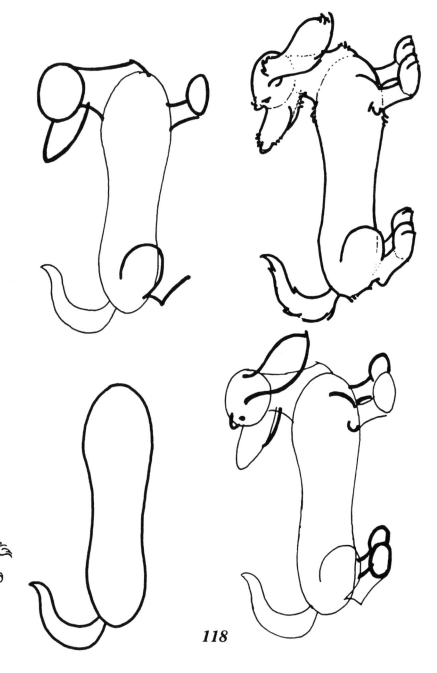

Write On!

Holidays

> "I've heard about H-H-Halloween," Howie stammered. "That's when the goblins come out to play. And the witches. And the ghosts and the ghouls."
>
> "Don't forget the skeletons," said Chester. "They'd be hurt to the bone if you left them out."
>
> —*from* Scared Silly: A Halloween Treat

> "Did Santa Claus bring all this stuff?" Howie asked, jumping down from Mrs. Monroe's arms. "And here I thought he used that bag to carry off bad puppies."
>
> "Merry Christmas, you guys," Toby shouted as he ran to us.
>
> —*from* The Fright Before Christmas

Howie is a young puppy, just finding out about holidays. Write about holidays on these pages.

My favorite holiday is _____

because: _____

_____

_____

My least favorite holiday is _____

because: _____

_____

The best present I ever *gave* was: _____

_____

The best present I ever *got* was: _____

_____

My favorite holiday song is: _____

My favorite holiday food is: _____

When I get older, this is a holiday tradition I'm going

  to keep observing: _____

_____

If I could make up my own holiday, I'd call it _____

_____

and hold it on _____ (date).

This is what my own holiday would be about: _____

_____

_____

_____

_____

Wacky Words!

Wacky Words! is a game that's fun for one person, two people, or the whole gang. If you're playing it alone, fill in the list on the next page with whatever words come to mind. Don't turn the page until you've completed the entire list. *Then* turn the page and fill in the blanks in the story, using the words you've listed here.

If you're playing with others, go directly to page 124. Announce the type of word called for under each blank. Each of the other players takes a turn providing a word that fits. Don't read any of the story aloud until all the blanks are filled in. Then read it from beginning to end—and just try to keep from laughing! The wackiest, funniest, and most descriptive words will give you the wildest, craziest stories!

Harold's Recipe

_____	_____
1. PLURAL NOUN	13. ADJECTIVE
_____	_____
2. FOOD	14. VERB
_____	_____
3. FOOD	15. NUMBER
_____	_____
4. LIQUID	16. ADJECTIVE
_____	_____
5. FOOD	17. NOUN
_____	_____
6. UNIT OF MEASUREMENT	18. NUMBER
_____	_____
7. VERB	19. ADJECTIVE
_____	_____
8. ADJECTIVE	20. NOUN
_____	_____
9. NOUN	21. VERB
_____	_____
10. NOUN	22. LIQUID
_____	_____
11. NUMBER	23. NUMBER
_____	
12. ARTICLE OF CLOTHING	

Wacky Words!

Harold's Recipe for Chocolate _____
(1. plural noun)

Ingredients

1 tablespoon _____
(2. food)

1 cup _____
(3. food)

2 cups _____
(4. liquid)

A pinch of _____
(5. food)

6 _____ chocolate
(6. unit of measurement)

The great thing about this recipe is that it's easy to

_____ and it tastes _____ !
(7. verb)   (8. adjective)

All you need is a spoon and a big _____ to mix
(9. noun)

everything in. Preheat your _____ to
(10. noun)

_____ degrees. Be sure to put on a(n)
(11. number)

124

_____ so you don't get all _____
(12. article of clothing) *(13. adjective)*

while baking. Mix all the ingredients together and

_____ for _____ minutes or until the
(14. verb) *(15. number)*

mixture appears to be getting _____ . Next,
(16. adjective)

grease a _____ so the batter doesn't stick. Pour
(17. noun)

out the batter and bake for _____ minutes. It
(18. number)

won't be long until a(n) _____ smell will fill the
(19. adjective)

air. Your _____ will be watering! Just give these
(20. noun)

chocolate treats a few minutes to _____ , then
(21. verb)

pour yourself a glass of _____ and dig in!
(22. liquid)

Recipe serves _____ people.
(23. number)

Harold's Chocolate Challenge

Harold says:

"Chester knows a lot—or at least he pretends to. He's always saying, 'Harold, let me tell you something.' Or, 'Harold, don't tell me you didn't know *that*!' One day I decided to prove that there's one thing I know more about than he does: CHOCOLATE! I put together this little challenge. I even made it easy for him. All he had to do was answer 'True' or 'False.' Well, he got most of the answers wrong and didn't speak to me for three days. But now that he's read the ten-volume *Encyclopedia of Chocolate*, he's the expert on everything again and feels much better.

   "Meanwhile, see how much you know about chocolate. If you don't know the answers, don't worry. You'll find everything you need to know on pages 128–129. Besides, you probably already know the only *important* fact about chocolate: It tastes great!"

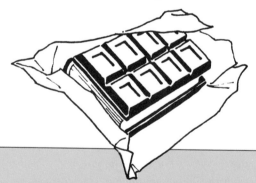

Safety Note

Harold is an unusual dog in many ways. He reads, he writes, and he loves chocolate. But chocolate is not a good food for most dogs; in fact, it makes them sick. Give your dog another kind of treat—one that's just right for him or her.

True or False

_____ **1.** The inventor of chocolate was named Xocoatl.

_____ **2.** At one time, cocoa beans were used as money.

_____ **3.** People have been eating chocolate since candy bars were invented by Milton S. Hershey in 1894.

_____ **4.** Baby Ruth candy bars were named for the great baseball player Babe Ruth.

_____ **5.** In the movie *E.T., The Extra-Terrestrial*, the boy Elliott leaves a trail of M&M's for E.T. to follow.

_____ **6.** The word "cocoa" means "food of the gods."

_____ **7.** A *truffle* is a kind of fungus.

_____ **8.** The first candy bar with a combination of ingredients was Snickers.

_____ **9.** White chocolate is not real chocolate.

_____ **10.** Chocolate causes cavities.

127

Answers to
Harold's
Chocolate Challenge

1. False   The inventor of chocolate was Mother Nature. However, for many centuries before anyone else had even discovered chocolate, the Aztec and Mayan people enjoyed a bitter-tasting drink made from crushed cocoa beans. This drink was called *xocoatl.*

2. True   Cocoa beans were the standard form of currency used by the ancient Aztecs and Mayans.

3. False   Milton S. Hershey manufactured the first American chocolate bars, the Hershey Almond Bar and the Hershey Milk Chocolate Bar, in 1894. However, so-called "eating chocolate" was first produced in 1847 by an English company called Fry & Sons. And milk chocolate was invented in 1876 by two Swiss chocolatiers, Daniel Peter and Henri Nestlé.

4. False   In 1920, Otto Schnering, president of the Curtiss Candy Company, named his new candy bar in honor of the daughter of former President Grover Cleveland.

5. False   When Mars Candies, the manufacturer of M&M's, was asked if their candy could be used in the movie, they said no. Why? Because they thought *E.T.*, one of the biggest movie successes of all time, would be a box-office flop. As a result, E.T. follows a path of Reese's Pieces instead of M&M's.

6. True Describing the cocoa tree, a mid-eighteenth-century botanist named Linnaeus said, "The fruit supplies the raw product for a most delicious, healthy, and nourishing drink." He gave the tree its name, "cocoa," which is derived from the Greek and does indeed mean "food of the gods."

7. True Wondering what this one has to do with chocolate? Well, a truffle is in fact a kind of underground fungus, considered a delicacy and eaten in salads. But there's a chocolate truffle as well. Made from the finest cocoa beans and the richest dairy cream, this kind of truffle is perhaps the most expensive and luxurious chocolate candy money can buy. It is certainly one of the most delicious!

8. False Snickers, with its combination of chocolate, caramel, peanuts, and nougat, is one of the most popular candy bars in America. It was first made by Mars Candies in 1930. Eighteen years earlier, however, in 1912, the Standard Candy Company of Nashville, Tennessee, introduced the Goo Goo Cluster Bar, with its combination of chocolate, caramel, marshmallow, and peanuts. The Goo Goo Cluster Bar is still going strong, but it is sold in only a few southern states.

9. True Technically, this is correct. White chocolate contains cocoa butter, but no chocolate liquor or cocoa solids. Its sweet taste is derived mostly from milk and vanilla.

10. False Chocolate actually contains a protein that blocks plaque and helps fight tooth decay. However, don't trade in your toothbrush for a candy bar. Nobody eats chocolate that doesn't have sugar added to it. And sugar, converted into acid by bacteria in the mouth, causes cavities.

Monster Hits!

Did you know that there really *were* hit songs called "The Monster Mash" and "The Purple People Eater"? And you've probably heard of the group The Grateful Dead. Here's your chance to come up with your own Top 5 Monster Hits. Make up songs that are funny, gruesome, or weird—and groups or performers who would be most likely to sing them.

	Song	Group/Performer
1.	_____	_____
	_____	_____
2.	_____	_____
	_____	_____
3.	_____	_____
	_____	_____
4.	_____	_____
	_____	_____
5.	_____	_____
	_____	_____

Famous Rabbits

Roger Rabbit

Roger Rabbit first appeared as a cartoon character in *Who Framed Roger Rabbit*, the 1988 hit movie that blended live action and animation. But did you know that he got his start in a book—not a children's book, but a humorous mystery for adults called *Who Censored Roger Rabbit?* written by Gary Wolf and published in 1981? Ten years later, Wolf wrote a sequel entitled *Who P-P-P-Plugged Roger Rabbit?* Although Wolf created Roger, the zany rabbit character went through many changes before appearing on the big screen. One of those changes was his height. Wolf had written him as being six feet tall! Among others who contributed to Roger's looks and personality were producer-director Steven Spielberg, the man who made *E.T., The Extra-Terrestrial* and many other box-office hits; directors Richard Williams and Robert Zemeckis (the latter also directed *Back to the Future*); and many talented animators in the United States and England. Roger's voice was created by actor Charles Fleischer.

Cat Crazy

Superstitions About Cats

🐾 In some Eastern European countries, cats were often locked out of doors during thunderstorms. This was done to protect houses against lightning. Why? Because it was believed that during storms, cats were possessed by demons, and the lightning that came from the heavens was being sent to exorcise them.

🐾 If cats were believed to be possessed by demons in some countries, in others they were thought to be able to drive demons away. In Russia, for instance, a cat was put into a new cradle to rid it of evil spirits before a baby was allowed to sleep in it.

🐾 Cats were often associated with the weather, and their behavior was thought to predict storms. In Scotland, as in many seafaring areas, a cat running about and clawing the furniture was taken as a sign that high winds were coming.

🐾 There have been many superstitions about cats aboard ships. In general, cats were considered good luck, especially black cats. However, in some cases where it was lucky to have a cat on board, it was extremely *unlucky* to say the word "cat."

🐾 It is still a common superstition in the United States that a black cat crossing one's path means that bad luck is sure to come. However, in England, black cats are thought to be lucky, and a black cat walking in front of a bride and groom is a very good omen. In America, a white cat is considered to be lucky. In England, a white cat is bad news. Why? Because white is the color of ghosts!

🐾 From Wales comes this superstition: When someone is ill, wash the patient and throw the water over a cat. Then shoo the cat out of the house, and it will take the illness with it.

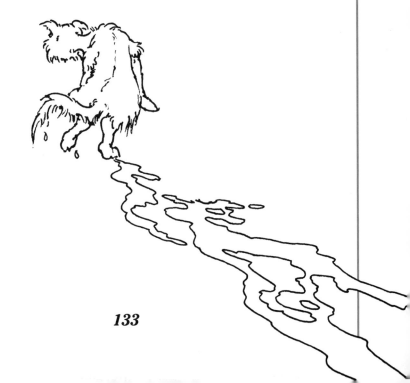

Word Find

Reining Cats and Dogs

The famous cats and dogs listed below starred in movies, plays, TV shows, cartoons, comic strips, and books. How many do you recognize? Can you find their names among the letters on the next page? Remember that the names may run from left to right or from right to left, from top to bottom or from bottom to top, or on a diagonal in either direction. But whichever way they go, the letters always follow a straight line.

Among these feline and canine celebrities are three of each species from the Bunnicula books. Can you identify them and name which books they appeared in?

The solutions appear on page 163.

CATS	DOGS
CHESTER	BENJI
FELIX	HAROLD
GARFIELD	HOWIE
KRAZY KAT	LASSIE
LYLE	MARMADUKE
PUSS IN BOOTS	MAX
RUM TUM TUGGER	OLD YELLER
SNOWBALL	PLUTO
SYLVESTER	RIN TIN TIN
THOMASINA	SNOOPY
TOM KITTEN	TOTO

```
P L U T A B N E A D L O R A H K
U U R E S N O O P Y I E E O X Y
S T A K Y Z A R K O G M W L D L
S O V U A B C T T G J E L Y L Z
I L W D O X T O U D O G L L E P
N D F A A S O T U L P R A V I E
B Y E M Y A M O H K I B S A F T
O E V R Y U K B Z O W Y S L R M
O L R A T E I Q M O M X I F A N
T L S M I T T E N K E A E E G A
S E U W R E T S E V L Y S L F B
S R O C A T E I Z B E N J I E N
A H O R R I N T I N T I N X N T
V U R E T S E H C T I N R I N A
```

Pencil Pause

Funny Face

Sometimes the hardest part about drawing is knowing where to begin. This page may not lend you a helping hand, but you *will* find plenty of noses, eyes, ears, warts, mouths, and other face parts to choose from! Find the ones you like best, and then draw them in your own hand onto the oval on the next page. Have fun . . . and remember, the weirder the face, the better!

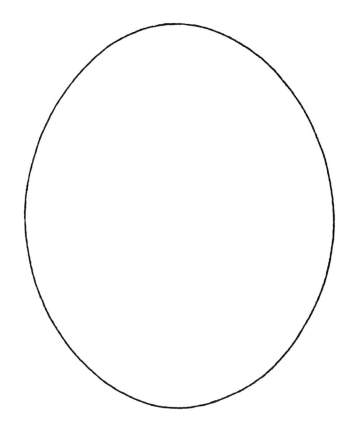

The Funniest!

The funniest thing I ever saw was: _____

_____

_____

The funniest thing that ever happened to me was: _____

_____

_____

The funniest thing that ever happened in class was: _____

_____

_____

The funniest way I ever dressed was: _____

_____

The funniest person I know is: _____

_____

The funniest thing about my best friend is: _____

_____

_____

The funniest movie I ever saw was: _____

_____

The funniest TV show I ever watched was: _____

_____

The funniest song I ever heard was: _____

_____

The funniest comic or cartoon character is: _____

_____

The funniest line of a book or movie I can remember is:

_____

_____

_____

Bunnicula's 20-Carrot Quiz

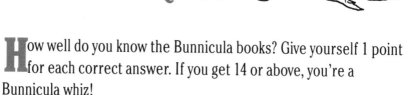

How well do you know the Bunnicula books? Give yourself 1 point for each correct answer. If you get 14 or above, you're a Bunnicula whiz!

The answers appear on page 164.

1. Chester suspects that Bunnicula is really a ⌇⎯⎯⎯⎯.

    a) witch   **c)** robot
    b) vampire   **d)** gym teacher

2. The town in which the Monroes live is called ⌇⎯⎯⎯.

    a) Centerville   **c)** Philadelphia
    b) Pleasantville   **d)** Moscow

3. Toby gets to stay up late on Friday nights to ⌇⎯⎯⎯.

    a) watch TV   **c)** read
    b) play Nintendo   **d)** sort his socks

4. Pete's weekend soccer coach is ⌇⎯⎯⎯.

    a) Mr. Monroe   **c)** Bunnicula
    b) Mrs. Monroe   **d)** none of the above

5. Chester thinks that Howie howls the way he does because Howie ⌇⎯⎯⎯.

    a) misses his parents
    b) has stomach problems
    c) is part werewolf
    d) likes to complain

6. Harold's very favorite food is ⌁⎯⎯⎯⎯.
- **a)** chocolate cupcakes with cream in the center
- **b)** cheeseburgers
- **c)** dog food with parsley sprinkled on top
- **d)** green sourballs

7. Chester enjoys reading books by ⌁⎯⎯⎯⎯.
- **a)** Edgar Allan Poe
- **b)** Charles Dickens
- **c)** Stephen King
- **d)** all of the above

8. Two characters who were guests at Chateau Bow-Wow in the book *Howliday Inn* make appearances in two later books. These two characters are ⌁⎯⎯⎯⎯.
- **a)** Taxi and Lyle
- **b)** Max and Georgette
- **c)** Ernie and Bert
- **d)** Howard and Heather

9. Toby is Pete's ⌁⎯⎯⎯⎯.
- **a)** older brother
- **b)** younger brother
- **c)** cousin
- **d)** goldfish

10. Bunnicula was found in a ⌁⎯⎯⎯⎯.
- **a)** cave
- **b)** library
- **c)** movie theater
- **d)** cemetery

11. In thinking of names for Bunnicula, the only one *not* suggested by a member of the Monroe family was ⌐.
   a) Mr. Johnson   **c)** Cecil
   b) Fluffy   **d)** Bun-Bun

12. The Monroes have a vacation house located ⌐ and named ⌐.
   a) at the beach ... Surfin' Safari
   b) on a lake ... Lake Expectations
   c) in the mountains ... Peak Experience
   d) in their backyard ... Cheap Getaway

13. Chester tries to get rid of Bunnicula by using all the following *except* ⌐.
   a) steak   **c)** bagels
   b) water   **d)** garlic

14. Howie first appears in the book ⌐.
   a) *Bunnicula*   **c)** *The Celery Stalks at Midnight*
   b) *Howliday Inn*   **d)** *Charlotte's Web*

15. Chester's favorite place to sleep is ⌐.
   a) on Harold's head
   b) on a rug in the front hall
   c) in a brown velvet armchair in the living room
   d) at the foot of Pete's bed

16. At the beginning of every book in the Bunnicula series is a note from ⌐.
   a) your mother
   b) the editor
   c) Chester
   d) The Society for the Prevention of Cruelty to Vegetables

17. Mr. and Mrs. Monroe's first names are 🥕.
- **a)** Patrick and Jennifer
- **b)** Matthew and Gunnar
- **c)** Robert and Ann
- **d)** Tweedledum and Tweedledee

18. All the following descriptions fit Bunnicula *except* 🥕.
- **a)** vegetarian
- **b)** the quiet type
- **c)** cage dweller *most* of the time
- **d)** college graduate

19. Bunnicula has never 🥕 in any of the books.
- **a)** gotten out of his cage
- **c)** spoken
- **b)** attacked a zucchini
- **d)** won a prize

20. Howie calls Harold and Chester 🥕.
- **a)** Pop and Uncle Chester
- **b)** Jason and Luke
- **c)** Uncle Harold and Uncle Chester
- **d)** Uncle Harold and Pop

Word Find

Movie Monsters

The actors named below have played monsters of one kind or another in the movies. Some made whole careers out of playing scary characters. For others, the monster role was a one-time deal. Can you find these actors' *last* names hidden among the letters on the next page? The names may run from left to right or from right to left, from top to bottom or from bottom to top, or on a diagonal in either direction. But whichever way they go, the letters always follow a straight line.

The solution appears on page 164.

Peter BOYLE	Elsa LANCHESTER
Ricou BROWNING	Michael LANDON
Lon CHANEY	Charles LAUGHTON
Ben CHAPMAN	Christopher LEE
Robert ENGLUND	Bela LUGOSI
Michael J. FOX	Fredric MARCH
George HAMILTON	William MARSHALL
Boris KARLOFF	Vincent PRICE
Michael KEATON	Max SCHRECK

If you want to find out more about these actors, see page 146.

```
O K M O N S T E E C I R P X
L E E L Y O B T N Y S L F E
L A R A E X Y N O Z O I B C
A T N O N F O F D I G G I T
H O Z C A T O F N E U M L L
S N W V H S Y K A R L O F F
R T I G C E N G L U N D I M
A B U L O A S C H R E C K A
M A H A M I L T O N O K E R
L N A M P A H C E S V U Y C
A U G G N I N W O R B O O H
```

About These
Movie Monsters

Max Schreck played the first movie Dracula (though the character was called Orlok) in the 1922 silent film *Nosferatu*. This movie is considered a classic. The actor's name, "Schreck," is the German word for "fright."

Lon Chaney played many monstrous characters in silent films, including the classic *Phantom of the Opera* in 1925. Makeup changed his features so completely in each new film that he was called the Man of a Thousand Faces. Chaney's son, **Lon Chaney, Jr.**, also made a career playing monsters, among them the title role in *The Wolf Man* in 1941.

Bela Lugosi is still the most famous movie Dracula. He played the part first on the Broadway stage, then in the 1931 movie *Dracula*. Nobody ever sent chills down as many spines as he did by simply announcing, "I . . . am . . . Count . . . Dracula."

Boris Karloff had a long acting career playing many parts, but was most famous for creating the role of the monster in the 1931 movie *Frankenstein*.

Fredric March won an Oscar for his performance in the 1932 film *Dr. Jekyll and Mr. Hyde*, based on the classic Robert Louis Stevenson story of good and evil.

Elsa Lanchester was "the bride of Frankenstein" in the 1935 movie of the same name. Her hairdo made her look as if she'd stuck her finger in an electrical outlet.

Charles Laughton was a great actor whose career included many brilliant performances, not the least of which was the title role in *The Hunchback of Notre Dame* in 1939.

Ricou Browning and **Ben Chapman** both played the "creature from the black lagoon" in the 1954 movie of that name. Chapman played the creature on land, while swimming champion Browning took over for the underwater sequences.

Michael Landon went on to star in the TV series *Bonanza* and *Little House on the Prairie* after playing the title role in *I Was a Teenage Werewolf* in 1957.

Vincent Price spent much of his career playing creepy characters and is associated with movie versions of the stories of Edgar Allan Poe, including *The Fall of the House of Usher* in 1960.

Christopher Lee became a star playing monsters, most notably Dracula, in a series of movies made by the British production company Hammer Films in the 1960s and 1970s.

William Marshall, a well-known stage actor, played an African prince attacked by Dracula during a visit to Transylvania and transformed into "Blacula" in the 1972 movie of that name.

Peter Boyle played the monster in the very funny 1974 spoof *Young Frankenstein*. The original movie monster had two bolts holding his head to his neck. This monster sported a zipper!

George Hamilton played Count Dracula in another spoof of the horror genre released in 1979, *Love at First Bite*.

Robert Englund played the terrifying Freddy Krueger in the 1984 horror film *Nightmare on Elm Street* and its many sequels.

Michael J. Fox, like Michael Landon, got his start in the movies as a teenage werewolf. Fox starred in the 1985 film *Teen Wolf*. Well-known for the popular TV series *Family Ties*, the actor had not yet made *Back to the Future*, the first of his many box-office hits.

Michael Keaton played the bioexorcist Betelgeuse in the popular 1988 horror-comedy *Beetlejuice*. Keaton is well-known for many other movie roles, of course, including the title character in *Batman* and *Batman Returns*.

Write On!

A Scary Story

> *"Tell us a ghost story, Pop."*
>
> *"Well, I don't know," Chester said. The leaves about us stirred in the wind. A branch snapped somewhere off to my left.*
>
> *"A scary story," Dawg said. "Yer good at that, Chester."*
>
> —*from* Nighty-Nightmare

Write a scary story on pages 151–154. A *really* scary story. A ghost story, perhaps. A Halloween story. The story of a haunted house . . . or a vampire . . . or a dark, dark night when the wind howled and you *thought* you were all alone.

If you think you'll need more paper than these pages, use the space here to get started or to jot down some ideas.

Here are some suggestions:

1. Don't make it all blood-and-guts. Try to make it a spine-tingly, skin-crawly, what's-going-to-happen-next story that uses suspense even more than shock.

2. After you've written it, imagine what kind of music and sound effects you could add to make it even scarier. You can get good sound effects records and tapes in many libraries. Or make your own creaking-door, howling-wind, moaning-ghost noises.

3. Now that you have your story, sound effects, and music, why not:

Act it out with friends for an audience.

OR

Record it on a tape recorder and play it for your family—with the lights off!

OR

Use a video camera to make your own horror movie.

You can also have fun making costumes and creating monster makeup and special effects.

_____

_____

_____

_____

_____

_____

_____

_____

_____

Answers

2 Help Bunnicula Get to the Salad Bowl

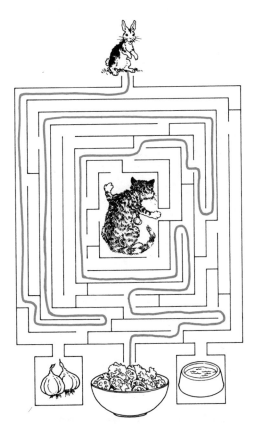

4 Chester's Magic Hat Puzzle

CLUES	**B**LEED
HANDS	**A**RGUE
ELVES	**T**ITLE
SNAKE	**T**OTAL
TEETH	**L**ARRY
EARTH	**E**LBOW
RAISE	
'	**C**LIMB
SEVEN	**R**IFLE
	YEARS

Chester's Battle Cry:

SAVE THE VEGETABLES!!

8 Bunnicula's Cousin?!

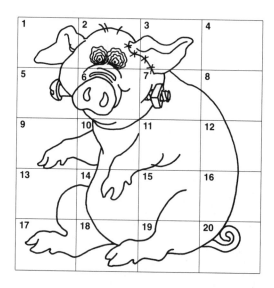

Frankenswine—Bunnicula's Cousin?!

156

30 Bunnicula's Crossword Puzzle

¹A	²S	K		³H			⁴C	A	⁵P	E	
	A		⁶B	O	⁷L	⁸T	⁹S			U	
	¹⁰V	A	M	P	I	R	E			¹¹T	¹²V
¹³B	E		W		¹⁴F	A	N	G	¹⁵S		E
¹⁶O	D	¹⁷D		¹⁸T	E	N	T		K		G
	X		¹⁹R	²⁰O	G		²¹S	E		²²I	²³C	E
	²⁴M	A	R	I	²⁵L	Y	N		²⁶N	O	T
²⁷C		F		²⁸F	A	L	C	²⁹O	N		A
³⁰A	³¹C	T	³²S		³³V	E	R	Y			B
³⁴L	A		³⁵I	³⁶O	³⁷W	A			³⁸A		L
³⁹F	R	A	N	K	E	N	S	⁴⁰W	⁴¹I	N	E
	R		G			I		⁴²I	N	N	S
	⁴³O	⁴⁴V	E	⁴⁵N		A		⁴⁶N	C		
⁴⁷S	T	A	R	E	S		⁴⁸A	S	H	E	S

48 Harold's Crossword Puzzle

1 S	2 H	A	3 G	■	4 S	P	5 A	N	6 I	7 E	8 L	9 S
10 T	I	■	11 R	12 A	P	■	P	■	13 T	R	I	P
■	■	14 C	A	N	I	15 N	E	■	■	16 A	T	E
17 W	■	18 H	Y	D	R	A	N	19 T	20 S	■	21 T	N
E	■	O	■	22 H	I	M	■	23 H	I	K	E	D
R	■	24 C	R	A	T	E	■	E	■	■	R	■
E	■	O	■	R	■	■	■	25 L	E	26 A	S	27 T
28 W	E	L	C	O	M	29 E	■	E	■	B	■	O
O	■	A	■	L	■	30 A	31 S	A	■	O	■	A
32 L	33 I	T	■	34 D	A	C	H	S	35 H	U	N	D
36 F	L	E	A	S	■	H	■	37 H	A	T	■	S

52 Harold's Magic Hat Puzzle

H ALF
A UNT
R EAD
O GRE
L OVE
D EAF
'
S ILO

D OOR
R AKE
E VEN
A CHE
M ORE

Harold's Dream:
FUDGE FOREVER!!

56 Harold's Brain Benders

1. Chester said, "Elementary, my dear Harold. He dropped his stamp into a box of dry cocoa mix."

2. "Elementary, my dear Harold," Chester said with a knowing smile. "The men are two of three triplets."

3. "Elementary, my dear Harold. It doesn't matter which piece of paper Toby takes. He'll look at it, then rip it into tiny shreds. After that, he'll say to Pete, 'Well, I know which candy bar is mine. Which one is yours?' Pete will have to show him the other piece of paper, on which the word 'little' will also be written. Pete will be caught in his own deception and have no choice but to give Toby the bigger bar."

68 Mixed-Up Animals

A. BUNNY	**1.** H	
B. LAMB	**2.** J	
C. FAWN	**3.** F	
D. CHICK	**4.** A	
E. TADPOLE	**5.** L	
F. OWLET	**6.** D	
G. KID	**7.** E	
H. PUPPY	**8.** P	
I. CUB	**9.** I	
J. KITTEN	**10.** Q	
K. CATERPILLAR	**11.** G	
L. GOSLING	**12.** K	
M. CALF	**13.** O	
N. DUCKLING	**14.** B	
O. EAGLET	**15.** N	
P. FOAL	**16.** M	
Q. CYGNET	**17.** C	

70 Young Animals Word Find

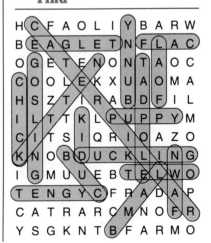

76 The House of Dr.E.A.D.

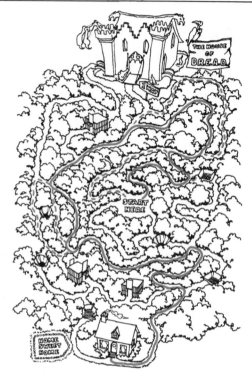

84 Creepy Creatures Word Find

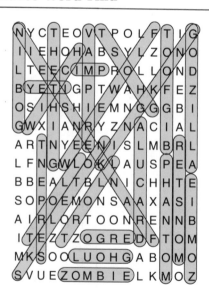

88 Itchy Witchy

Itch Witch

1. bat hat
2. ghost toast
3. beast feast
4. dull skull
5. broom room
6. mask task
7. bite fright
8. weird beard
9. ghoul tool
10. rich witch

Itchy Witchy

1. scary fairy
2. level devil
3. gory story
4. bony phony
5. shiver giver
6. phantom bantam
7. witch's riches
8. candle handle
9. creature teacher
10. spider cider

96 Chester's Crossword Puzzle

¹P	A	■	²T	³O	■	⁴B	R	⁵O	T	H	⁶E	R
A	■	⁷D	A	W	⁸G	■	I	■	H	■	L	■
⁹S	¹⁰H	E	R	L	O	C	K	H	O	¹¹L	¹²M	E	S
¹³T	O	T	■	■	S	■	E	■	¹⁴H	A	R	M
A	■	¹⁵E	¹⁶H	■	¹⁷S	¹⁸D	■	¹⁹C	■	Z	■	²⁰E	²¹X
■	■	²²C	U	²³R	I	O	S	I	T	Y	■	²⁴N	Y
²⁵C	²⁶A	T	N	I	P	■	■	R	■	■	T	■
²⁷A	L	I	G	N	■	²⁸F	■	²⁹C	A	³⁰T	N	A	³¹P
³²L	I	V	E	S	■	³³I	L	L	■	O	■	³⁴R	R
L	■	³⁵E	R	E	C	T	■	³⁶E	V	E	R	Y	■

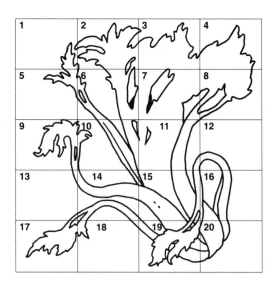

V-V-VVeggie-Vampires?!

104 Opening Lines

1. *J*
2. *B*
3. *F*
4. *D*
5. *A*
6. *E*
7. *G*
8. *C*
9. *I*
10. *H*

116 Howie's Crossword Puzzle

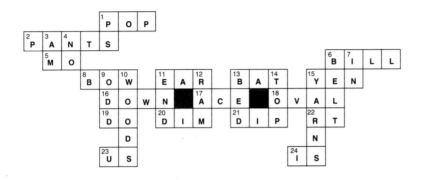

134 Reining Cats and Dogs Word Find

Did you recognize these characters from the Bunnicula books?

Cats

Chester—all the books

Lyle—*Howliday Inn*

Snowball—*The Celery Stalks at Midnight*

Dogs

Harold—all the books

Howie—all the books except *Bunnicula* and *Howliday Inn*

Max—*Howliday Inn* and *The Celery Stalks at Midnight*

1. *b*

2. *a*

3. *c*

4. *b*

5. *c*

6. *a*

7. *d*

8. *b*—Max reappeared in *The Celery Stalks at Midnight*, and Georgette showed up in *Return to Howliday Inn*

9. *b*

10. *c*

11. *c*

12. *b*

13. *c*

14. *b*

15. *c*

16. *b*

17. *c*

18. *d*

19. *c*

20. *d*

144 Movie Monsters Word Find